# THE UGLY POPCORN TREE

## It Did What?!

By Madelyn Rohrer

ISBN 978-0-692083536

Cover design: Jerry Paulsen
www.designs.jerrypaulsen.com

www.storytellermadelynrohrer.com

This book is dedicated to orphans, adoptees, foster children, foster parents, and adoptive parents. It is dedicated to all of the teachers, medical personnel, and other caregivers who interface with children – those who <u>can</u> make a difference and do.

Thank you to my contributors and proofreaders:

Betty Calliham
Victoria Ingalls
Carole Marks
Jerry Paulsen
Howard Rohrer

# Introduction

Our "growing up years" –

As storytellers, we enjoy the opportunity to tell others about special people who have made a difference in the formative years of our lives – those who have influenced us and helped us to become the people we are today. Most of the time our stories will be about people close to us – a parent, grandparent, teacher, minister, a neighbor or a friend.  Other times, we might tell about a more remote person such as a movie hero or an historic figure...someone with charisma or characteristics we wish we had; someone we wanted to be like when we grew up.

Then there are those in the background of our lives who briefly appear and disappear, but leave behind a thought or a few words embedded forever into our minds and hearts – people whose casual words or actions may have unknowingly caused us to veer from our intended path or think differently about our future. Most of us have memories of those people, although we may or may not even remember their names. They might not remember our names. They may never know that they changed a young person's life with just a few simple words of encouragement.

"Words" are so important, especially to young people. They can build up or tear down. But the most important words of all are the ones that encourage, create a smile, spark an interest, or cause a child to want to know more – igniting the desire to try harder, to be all he or she was meant to be.

"The Ugly Popcorn Tree" is about orphans – children outside of a normal family environment, and the adults who affect their lives. It is a fictional story with fictional characters but based on true-to-life feelings and experiences of displaced children, especially older ones. Not all orphans will be fortunate enough to be in the care of a "Mrs. Rose;" many will not even survive the streets. But sometimes adversity makes a person stronger. The success of many notable personalities has proven that to be true (see pages 89-90). They rose above their circumstances to become not only successful, but good role models. Perhaps they met someone early in their lives who made a difference by offering those few words of kindness, hope, or encouragement.

*Madelyn Rohrer*

All of the historical information contained herein has been documented and verified with at least three separate sources.

# Table of Contents

# How it All Began

Decorating! Oh, no! Ugh! Marty slid down in his chair and looked away, hoping that Mrs. Rose would not notice him...wishing that somehow he could just become invisible.

"Special announcements" at the Barclay Children's Home usually meant activities outside the normal schedule posted on the bulletin board. Most of the time they were exciting, or at least interesting, but not this one – not as far as Marty was concerned.

Mrs. Rose, the administrator, told them that this year, for the very first time, the annual Christmas Tree Decorating Contest at the Maltby Tree Farm was going to be open to <u>all</u> children's groups in the community – not just an event for the local Boys Club and Girls Club. She said she had just spoken with Mrs. Maltby who confirmed that their orphanage would definitely be considered an eligible children's group. All they had to do to enter the contest was fill out a form with the name of their organization and list the names and ages of the children who would be participating.

"There are no assignments," she said, smiling, as she looked over at Marty. "It is all voluntary."

With a sigh of relief, Marty sat back up.

He was the oldest kid at Barclay. At twelve years old, he had assumed the role of a big brother to the younger children, often helping new arrivals adjust to their unfamiliar surroundings. He had been at Barclay Children's Home all his life and knew he was going to be there until he was officially an adult at age 18, or perhaps a little longer if he was still attending school. He let go of the typical orphan's dream of being adopted years ago – those hopes were gone. He used to feel bad about being overlooked by prospective parents time after time, but not anymore. He was realistic.

*Why would anyone choose to bring home a kid like me with crooked teeth, yucky red, almost orange hair, skin covered with freckles, and an Adams Apple that bounces up and down when I talk? No one*, he reasoned. *I can't do anything about the way I look and I can't do anything about my age. People who come here are looking for cute babies or preschoolers. Nobody wants an ugly kid of any age...not even my real parents! They left me on the front porch of the orphanage in an orange crate!*

Marty saw the note they left – it was pasted in the back of a scrapbook that Mrs. Rose kept for him, along with a picture she took when they brought him inside. It said: "Please take care of Marty. He is a good baby but we cannot keep him." The orphanage took him in, figuring him to be about a week old. Mrs. Rose wrote his arrival date on the back of the picture: July 3, 1942. His name became Marty L. Smith. The "L" didn't stand for anything; it was just an initial in case he needed one.

This was his home and his life.

Now, being an older child, Marty was allowed to have a few off-premises assignments. His favorite was picking up the day-old newspaper from Schultz's Barber Shop around the corner. It was an assignment that he eagerly accepted as a privilege. He read a lot, and especially enjoyed reading the newspaper. He liked knowing what was going on in his town and the country, even the world. Yeah, the news was a day old and the pages were sometimes a little ragtag after being read by Mr. Schultz's customers, but it was free. Once, when there was no one in the barber shop, Mr. Schultz even gave Marty a free Grapette™ soda and let him sit in the barber's chair and read the current news of the day just like a real customer. He didn't actually get a haircut though; it was just pretend. Mrs. Rose always cut his hair.

Today was starting out a little different. The news in yesterday's paper about the tree decorating contest was stirring up considerable excitement in the orphanage, but Marty had absolutely no interest in anything that had to do with decorating. He simply didn't like it. He would rather help *build* a wall than have to decide what color to paint it or where to hang a picture. He wanted nothing to do with decorating a wall, a tree, or anything else!

But he did read about it when he got back from the barber shop. The local section of the newspaper covered the contest every year with pictures of the happy winners from the Boys Club and Girls Club. These were two separate organizations for kids in the area who got together every day after school and sometimes on weekends. The clubs began during World War II, mostly for kids whose parents were both working or whose fathers were off fighting in the war and whose mothers were working. No one at Barclay belonged to the clubs because they cost money; no one in the orphanage had money.

While Mrs. Rose left for a few minutes, Marty read the article again. The tree decorating contest was started by William and Maria Maltby, the newspaper reported, originally intended to be a wartime morale-booster for the children at the two clubs where Maria was a volunteer. As she spent time with the young people, she sensed their loneliness...separated from military fathers month after month and deprived of attention from mothers who were working in factories to support the war effort as well as their families. In 1944, after Maria's wounded army husband returned home to recuperate from his injuries, they talked about what they could do to help other families in the community who were still impacted by war. They thought about a tree decorating contest because they had a tree farm and it was almost Christmas. It was something that they could do personally for the kids – something that would take their minds off the war for a while.

"What a joy it was that first year," Maria said in the article, "to see the excitement and camaraderie of the children as they showed up in teams with their decorations and plans. We didn't have much to offer in the way of prizes, but we made sure each child got a little gift, even if it was just a comic book or a piece of candy. It was fun and the children have looked forward to it every year since."

Maria was asked about her own experiences while her husband was in the military. "How did you manage the tree farm, your home, and working a shift at the factory making parts for army vehicles? How did you find time to volunteer?"

"I just did what I could whenever I could," she replied. "The farm didn't require a lot of upkeep. While William was gone, I planted seedlings only when we had lots of rain and the ground was soft. That made the job easy because I could heel them in by myself. It took a little longer than when we were both doing the planting, but that was okay; the job got done. The house didn't take much work, especially when I was the only one living there. As for working at the factory, that was the *real priority* – it had to be! I was only one of many women who were doing what was necessary to keep those parts moving out the door for the war effort. Spending time at the Girls Club and Boys Club when they needed help was pure enjoyment for me. I gave them whatever time I could, mostly just a couple of hours each day after my shift was up at the factory and on weekends."

Maria was asked what led to the decision to expand the contest to an area-wide event. "Is it because this is your 10th anniversary?"

"Not totally. After William came back home and had time to heal, we continued to enlarge the growing areas of our farm. Now we have an abundance of all sizes of evergreens. Although we have always enjoyed doing things for children, this is the first year we felt that we had enough tall trees for a community-wide decorating contest and still have enough to cut for Christmas tree sales. So we decided to make our 10th anniversary contest special by opening it up to as many children's groups as want to participate... the Boys Club, Girls Club, 4-H, scouting groups, the elementary school, Sunday school classes, and more. It is going to be a big event with dozens of prizes. Plus, every child who enters will receive candy, so *everyone* will be a winner. We've also recently opened a gift shop where we sell locally crafted items made of wood. Some of these will be given away as prizes for the winners. Plus, we have created special 10th anniversary plaques for the organizations with the winning teams."

The theme was different every year. The newspaper listed the themes of past contests, with the first one appropriately being red, white and blue. Marty remembered the last five. There was a year of "Shaped Ornaments" – circles, squares, triangles, octagons. Then there was a year of "Animals," especially ones that would have been around the manger. Another was "Earth and Sky": trees, flowers, clouds, stars, Zodiac signs, etc. "Pennsylvania" was another theme; "Railroads" was another. This year, it was "Popcorn" – popcorn ornaments of any color, size or shape, popcorn pictures, and popcorn garland.

*** 

The Maltby Tree Farm was not new to Marty. Being one of the older kids at Barclay, he was assigned to the team that picked out a Christmas tree each year for their recreation room. The Maltbys always gave them a complimentary tree…any one they wanted, as long as they could load it onto their vehicle and get it back to the orphanage themselves. There was no delivery service for Christmas trees. Then they had to unload it from the roof of their station wagon, maneuver it down the hallway, through the rec room door, and get it sitting up straight in the tree stand. That was when Marty was finished. All the children were invited to help decorate, of course, but he was never interested in that part of the process – that was for girls and little kids! Getting the tree from the farm to the rec room stand was the extent of his involvement.

Then *why* was he having this feeling of uneasiness today? He shrugged it off. *Probably because all the little kids are getting excited about entering this goofy contest,* he reasoned. Then he sighed. *That means we'll probably all have to be involved somehow!* But that's just the way it was at Barclay Children's Home – kids helping kids!

He put the newspaper back on the rec room table as the meeting was being reconvened. Mrs. Rose announced that she now had a copy of the official instructions for the contest. Excitement was building! Marty tried to make it look as though he was paying attention because it was the polite thing to do. They were taught to always be polite to one another. Silently, however, he was tuning it out. He forced his mind to think about other things – *any* other things! In spite of his efforts, he found himself half-listening.

1) Age categories were 5-7, 8-10, and 11-12.

   That would include about a dozen kids at Barclay, Marty quickly calculated. The others were preschoolers.

2) Entrants had to sign up as teams, with four children per team, all in the same age group.

   *Oh, no!* Suddenly, it hit him; he <u>had</u> to pay attention now! Barclay only had four kids in the 11-12 age range: two 11-year-old twins – Mitch and Hannah, another 12-year-old – Joel, and himself. It meant that Barclay could only have a team in the 11-12 age category if all four chose to participate. He glanced over at the other three. They were not only listening rather intently, they were occasionally looking over at him! Once again, he wanted to disappear.

3) Decorations had to be handmade – nothing store bought.

   No problem there – kids at the orphanage didn't have money of their own, nor did they have any way of earning it. Only the staff got paid.

4) The theme this year was "Popcorn." Winners would be judged by how well they used popcorn in their decorations.

   Now THAT could be a problem. Popcorn was a once-a-week treat at Barclay. He couldn't imagine any kid wanting to give up his or her popcorn so it could be covered with paste and shaped into balls or bells or whatever and hung on a tree. Girls, maybe, but probably not any of the guys – and *for sure* not him.

5) There would be two judged categories: The Most Beautiful Popcorn Tree plus The Most Creative Popcorn Tree. Prizes would be given to each member of the winning team in each category *and in each age group.*

   Marty did another quick calculation. *Wow, that's two judged categories times three age groups times four kids on each team...twenty-four prizes!* And the prizes that Mrs. Rose read off *were* impressive! They could choose from some pretty good stuff – a 6-seater toboggan, a 4-seater sled, a short sled for one person, or a large snow saucer that could hold two adults or three kids. There were wooden hockey sticks, baseball bats, doll cradles, and jewelry boxes, all beautifully polished and painted, hand-crafted by local people and sold in the gift shop at the Maltby farm.

6) Every child who entered would have their choice of a large candy cane, maple sugar candy, or ribbon candy. Everyone was a winner of something!

Marty was *almost* tempted to think about it for the sake of the other three kids...almost. Nah! "Beautiful" and "creative" were two words he would never use in describing anything he did or anything he was. Trying to be attractive in any way was just not him; it was pretending to be someone else. He had tried a couple of times to make himself look better, but it always led to rejection and he had enough rejection in his life. *Besides, it sounds like a lot of work for a dumb piece of candy,* he justified.

But it was the last bit of information that did get Marty's attention. The town newspaper was going to sponsor an additional category with a special prize of its own. They were calling it "The Ugliest Popcorn Tree." The prize was a month's supply of popcorn for a whole family (a full pound for every day), including butter, and even some cheese and caramel that could be melted for drizzling! Now THAT sounded interesting! He knew there was no way he could win a prize for making something look beautiful, and he was definitely not creative, but he did know a lot about ugly! And wouldn't the kids in the orphanage enjoy all that popcorn with butter and cheese and caramel. That would be a real treat!

The thought was short-lived as his sense of reality kicked back in. *What if we don't win? Then it's just a big disappointment and a lot of time wasted for a piece of candy. Nah, it's a dumb idea.*

Oh, no! Hannah, Mitch, and Joel, the other "oldsters," were walking toward him.

# THE UGLY POPCORN TREE

# *Getting Ready*

Mitch and Joel thought ugly was cool – they weren't very good at making anything fancy either. The lone female, Hannah, didn't have a chance. It was three against one if they were going to enter the contest at all. She agreed to "turn off the pretty side of her brain," as Mitch politely suggested, and think ugly. They filled out their entry form and turned it in to Mrs. Rose. But thinking ugly wasn't as easy as they thought it would be.

After three afternoons of sitting around the kitchen table with paper and pencils, staring at their brown bag of unpopped corn and discarding one idea after another, they were getting discouraged.

"Maybe we should change direction and try for the creative award," Hannah suggested hopefully. Once again, she was outvoted. The only thing they agreed on was that they didn't want to pop their allotment until they figured out what they were going to do with it.

"Maybe we could paint the tree black to begin with," said Joel. "I know there's a can of black paint out in the shed. Or maybe tar would be gooier and uglier. There's a can of tar out there, too. We could thin it out a bit and let it run down through the branches. Or maybe we could do both."

"Nah - We wouldn't be allowed to goop up one of Maltby's trees," Mitch reasoned, "but *we could* paint the popcorn black and string it. Maybe we could even pull down some cobwebs from the shed and hang them on the tree for a better effect."

"Guys! This is supposed to be a Christmas tree, not a Halloween tree," Hannah reminded them with a bit of exasperation in her voice. "We need to stay focused on Christmas, or at least *something* with more cheerful colors. Our tree has to be ugly, not scary."

Hannah was right, they agreed. Nothing scary – just ugly. They thought about making red and green popcorn balls with nails sticking out of them – sharp ends pointing out, of course. They considered eggshells with strips of red popcorn hanging from them like tongues, maybe with black sticks stuck on the ends that looked like pieces of a wrought iron fence.

"Not a good idea," said Joel. "Some goofy kid would probably cut himself or go looking for a wrought iron fence to see if his tongue would really stick to it."

Again, they agreed. They shouldn't promote anything dangerous. Other ideas were really smelly socks filled with lumps of popcorn "coal" or perhaps popcorn reindeer covered with chimney soot. Once again, Hannah reminded them to think brighter.

"I thought we were," said Mitch. "White egg shells with red tongues seemed pretty bright to me. Okay, how about a popcorn Santa Claus that got too close to his reindeer's horns and got tossed into a tree and had red gashes on his arms with blood running down? We'd have to use real blood," he added. "Popcorn would soak up water colors and red would turn pink. No one has pink blood. Real blood sure would be ugly – and bright!"

The other boys agreed, except no one was willing to donate their blood. Hannah just shook her head. They were running out of ideas.

Marty stared at the ceiling, allowing his common-sense, reality thinking to kick in: *How can anything that has to do with Christmas possibly be ugly? Christmas is beautiful…everything about Christmas is beautiful. How can an evergreen tree be ugly, especially the ones on Maltby's farm? They are all pruned to perfection. It can be unadorned, but that doesn't make it ugly. If it is broken to pieces, burned or destroyed, that would make it ugly. Probably the Maltbys might have something to say about that,* he thought with a chuckle. *Nope – Christmas and trees cannot be decorated in any way and be made ugly. Overdone maybe, but never ugly.*

Then he thought about the opposite scenario; he thought about himself. *I am already ugly. I know from experience that every time I've tried to dress up I looked weird. I am what I am and there is no way to change. So that means pretty is pretty, and ugly is ugly,* he concluded. *There is no way you can decorate something that is pretty such as Christmas or a tree and make it into something ugly any more than you can decorate something ugly and make it into something pretty. It just can't happen. We are wasting our time! This whole idea is dumb!*

Then it hit him! "Wait a minute! I've got it!" he shouted suddenly to his surprised team. "Think about this! The facts are..." he continued in his most adult-sounding voice, "we cannot make Christmas into something ugly. It is impossible because everything about Christmas is beautiful. We can't convert a Christmas *tree* to ugly either – trees are beautiful whether they are decorated or not. The only thing that can *possibly* be ugly, therefore, is the popcorn itself – if we don't change it – *if we don't pop it!* We've been assuming that our popcorn has to be popped. That would make it fluffy and pretty. Well, that is, unless we mold it into something gory. But what is pretty about plain old popcorn kernels? Nothing. So, all we have to do is think of a way to put them on the tree just like they are – unpopped! Then we will have a truly ugly popcorn tree!"

Mitch, Joel, and Hannah just stared at him...and then back at each other as they thought about Marty's sensible conclusion. He was right!

Well, they could glue the kernels onto pieces of paper or little thin boards, maybe in some kind of weird design ornaments. They would definitely be ugly. On the other hand, they would also be boring. Is boring the same thing as ugly? No, they decided. Surely someone else would come up with the idea of using unpopped kernels and maybe theirs would be less boring – maybe. They kept thinking.

Their brainstorming session was interrupted by Bessie the cook. She needed the kitchen table to start preparing dinner. They began to move away when Hannah noticed the roll of brown baking paper Bessie set on the table.

"Hey, guys, could we do something with this," she asked as she lifted one edge of the paper? They all hesitated.

"Like what?" Marty asked.

"Like this." She tore off a piece of the paper and rolled it into a ball with her hands. "Instead of flat ornaments, we could make ball ornaments out of this, cover them with paste until they're really yucky, and stick the kernels on them or, better yet, stick *burnt* kernels onto them. Then we could tie them to the tree with string – or maybe twine would be better. There is nothing pretty or fancy about baking paper, unpopped popcorn, and plain old brown twine."

"Burnt kernels? How do you burn kernels without popping them?" Joel asked.

"Good point," replied Hannah, thoughtfully. "Maybe your idea of the black paint would be better."

Suddenly, Hannah looked as cool as one of the guys to Marty. "I like that idea of the paper balls, Hannah. It's got my vote. The black paint, too."

*Let's do it*, they all decided!

With a large chunk of Bessie's baking paper, a bottle of glue, a roll of twine, scissors, and their bag of popcorn, they moved their base of operations to the rec room table. It was on the opposite side of the room from where the little kids were busy at their short table. They were coloring paper rings to hook together as garlands

15

for the Barclay Christmas tree and were very happy using just a dab of glue on each ring. The oldsters knew they had to be careful. They didn't want the young ones getting the idea that more glue...*much more* glue meant more fun.

"Can you imagine what would happen if those kids saw us spreading glue on a piece of paper and then rolling it up into a ball with our bare hands?" Joel chuckled. "Can't you just see wads of gooey coloring paper flying through the air and stuck on hands and clothes or in someone's hair? Or worse yet, the walls?"

The vision elicited quiet laughter but also awareness of their surroundings. They didn't want to spend the rest of the evening washing up sticky kids and floors. They found an empty shoe box for holding the creations as they got them made and placed it on the top shelf of a nearby bookcase. It was time to get to work.

Hannah started to cut pieces from the paper but Mitch intervened. "Wouldn't it be uglier if we just tore off chunks of paper rather than cutting them out neatly," he asked? "Then we could make the balls different sizes. Maybe some of the rough ends might stick out, too." Another good idea!

"Wait," said Joel. "If we are going to roll this stuff into balls and cover them with kernels, why don't we make them into eyeballs instead of ornaments? The black kernels could be the pupils." Now that was a great idea, they decided! A tree full of eyeballs would really be ugly.

Finally...they were on a roll!

Now it was Marty's turn. "Hold on. Brown paper with brown and black kernels and brown twine is going to be really dull. How about if we actually pop some of the popcorn, crush it to semi-cover the paper balls which will make them less sticky, and add some hair like eyebrows? That would lighten up the ornaments and they would still look rough."

"Where are we going to get hair, Marty?" Joel asked. "We just brushed Barnie yesterday and cleaned out the doggie brush. His extra hair is all gone. Who's going to donate their hair?"

"I know exactly where to get it – Schultz's Barber Shop. I'll be going there in the morning."

"Hey, guys. I've got another thought," Hanna piped in. "We're worried that our décor will be boring, right? Well, maybe when we glue the crushed popcorn over the brown paper and stick some kernels on for pupils, we could run a little red food coloring down some of them like bloodshot eyes. Food coloring wouldn't mush into the popcorn like water paint. We could use an eyedropper; we wouldn't need much. It would make the eyeballs seem more real plus brighten up the tree and it would still be ugly. What do you think?"

"Brilliant, Hannah. Positively brilliant! Then do we need the hair or not?" asked Marty.

Hannah pondered for a moment and then lit up like a light bulb just went on. "Yes! Picture this: We will make some of the eyeballs look like normal eyeballs without hair and we will make them looking up toward a star on top of the tree. We will make all the other eyeballs either covered over with hairy eyebrows or bloodshot – or both. Remember our lesson from Sunday school last week where the wise men and the shepherds saw the star but others didn't? The other people didn't see it because they either didn't believe in a Messiah or didn't want to listen. The ones with clear eyes will be the believers and the ones with the hairy bloodshot eyes will be the unbelievers. Then we could put a sign on our tree that says, 'Looking for the Star.' Of course, we will have to make a star for the top. Maybe we could even make a manger out of this brown paper and fill it with unpopped kernels to give it some weight and set it kind of high in the branches. How does that sound?"

Whoa! Marty realized he was almost starting to feel excited about this whole thing. Never had ugly sounded so beautiful! He couldn't wait to get over to Schultz's Barber Shop in the morning. No, better yet, he would do it right now before Mr. Schultz closed for the day! "You guys go ahead and start popping some of the popcorn. Mitch – why don't you take some of the kernels out to the shed and paint them black. We don't need a lot for just the pupils. I'll be right back with the hair." He hurried out the door and returned twenty minutes later with a bag full of hair from Mr. Schultz's waste can. "He said we can have more tomorrow if we need it, but I think this will be enough."

They never could have imagined how tough it would be trying to glue loose snips of hair to crushed popcorn without first getting it stuck to their fingers. It was trial and error deciding what should come first – the hair or the glue. Marty went back to the barber shop the next day and emptied the waste can again.

Two days later they were finished – the proud owners of 30 "regular" white eyeballs with black pupils and 37 hairy-browed eyeballs with either black pupils or yellowish-brown ones – yellowish brown because they ran out of black paint and had to use some of the natural colored corn. Fifteen of the hairy eyeballs were bloodshot. The odd number was Joel's idea – no reason – it just seemed like a cool thing to do.

They found a large piece of tin in the shed and decided it would make a sturdy star for the top of their tree. While Marty and Mitch were busy drawing out a pattern, Joel poked them and whispered: "Look at Hannah. What is she doing?"

They weren't sure, but she was very engrossed in moving all the eyeballs in their two shoe boxes around, putting some of them out on the table for a while and then putting them back into the boxes...apparently in some kind of order. Mitch finally got up the courage to ask.

"I'm matching them up," she replied nonchalantly. "They have to go together in pairs and we won't have time to do it on Saturday. We can't have pairs of eyes with eyebrows that don't match."

"Why not?" Asked Mitch, trying to squelch a smile. "Would that be weird?"

"Of course it would," she answered without looking up from her work. "How would you like to have one blond eyebrow and one black one, or one curly one and one straight one?"

"Yeah, you're right. That would be downright ugly!"

There was silence for a few seconds as Hannah continued her sorting. Then she stopped, turned around, and looked at the trio grinning back at her. They all laughed. "I did it again, didn't I?" she admitted.

"Yup, wrong side of the brain."

The tin star came out perfect...just hefty enough to hold all the kernels they pasted on both sides without buckling, but not so heavy that it would be difficult to place in the short branches on top of a tree. They covered a small section in the middle of the star with white paint because Hannah said the middle of the star should be brighter than the edges. She didn't explain why and no one knew any different, so that's what they went with.

They made a 10-inch-long manger with the rest of the tin rather than brown paper because the brown paper sagged. They bent the ends up all around and attached the twine by wrapping it around the bent ends. It looked more like a hanging cradle than a manger so Hannah wrote "MANGER" on the front of it with glue and popcorn kernels. "We will need more kernels to fill the manger," she noted. "Otherwise we will have to use stones. We don't know how windy it will be on Saturday and we don't want it to blow away." Mrs. Rose allotted them another bag.

They were ready! All four were fired up with high hopes of winning the prize for the ugliest popcorn tree! But if they didn't win, they promised each other they would not be disappointed. They would think positive. They might not win a month's worth of gourmet popcorn with butter, cheese and caramel to share with the kids at Barclay, but they could still bring back whatever candy they got to divvy up for the preschoolers who couldn't participate. There would be enough for everyone.

# *The Contest*

Saturday morning started out chilly – typical for a December day in Pennsylvania, but there was no wind and the sun was shining, making it feel warmer than it really was. The Maltby Tree Farm was bustling with dozens of kids from 5 to 12, almost giddy with excitement as they were given their assigned team numbers and trees, then tackling their decorating missions with zeal. Every team was given the same kind of tree – just different heights, according to the age range of the team. With branches that spread out at the ends like little shelves rather than growing more upright, attaching ornaments and signs was easy. The sunshine and brilliant blue sky reflected sparkles as decorations were unpacked.

Barclay Children's Home entered three teams, one in each age group:

The 5-to-7-year-olds, with a little direction from Mrs. Rose, included a sign on their tree: "If I had a family, they would look like..." They made ornaments that looked like mothers and fathers, sisters and brothers, grandparents, dogs, cats, and even a horse and a parakeet.

The 8-to-10-year-olds chose combat figures. They did cut-outs of tanks, planes, ships, grenades, soldiers and sailors, covered them with crushed popcorn and painted them. Some of the ornaments were quite large, like the tanks and ships, so they had fewer than most, but they were well done and very creative.

When all the decorations were out of the van and situated near the correct trees, Mr. Rose found a comfortable bench mid-way between the two younger teams. No one was allowed to help decorate other than the children on the teams, so he just sat and watched with amusement as his young charges busily flitted around their trees. The sun was chasing away the chill, but he still gratefully accepted a cup of hot coffee from one of the Maltbys' helpers.

Marty, Mitch, Hannah, and Joel, the 11- and 12-year-olds from Barclay, were Team 17. They were around the corner and out of sight of Mr. Rose, something that didn't happen very often. They unpacked their ornaments and got down to business with a pre-planned strategy.

The star had to be put in place first. Being a team of the oldest kids, they had one of the taller trees, but it was just a little too tall to place the star on top without a ladder. The top of their tree had "prongs" that would be perfect to hold their relatively heavy star...if they could just get it up there! Not a problem. Marty and Joel joined their arms together for Hannah to stand on and balance while Mitch handed her the star. It took just a few seconds and nestled beautifully into place. There was no right side up they decided so whatever way it landed was perfect.

Next was the manger. They agreed on the best branch, which was about a foot down from the star and off to the right. Marty, being the tallest, placed it with ease, gently jostling it just enough to settle the kernels and keep it secure. There was no wind so they didn't have to tie it down.

Next came the signs. They had two of them: "Looking for the Star" was placed on the same level as the manger, directly under the star. "What Star?" was centered directly under the other sign but closer to the bottom of the tree.

Distribution of the eyeballs was not left to chance. They had a drawing of a tree in three sections for the perfect mix. The plain ones were placed around the upper part of the tree, pupils looking upward, with a clear view of the star. The hairy-browed bloodshot ones were in the middle, pupils looking down, as if refusing to see the star. They were spread out evenly to add just the right touch of color to the center of the tree. The extra eyeball was added to one of these, so one person right in the middle had three eyes. The hairy-browed clear eyes were toward the bottom, looking straight out, oblivious to the star.

Team 17 stood back and assessed their creation. Sixty-seven eyeballs hanging on a tree was definitely ugly at first glance, but after reading the signs and looking up at the star, they felt the message was perfectly clear. They rearranged a couple sets of eyes. Tree 17 was finished!

After checking in with Mr. Rose and then assessing Barclay's other two teams who were just finishing up and doing fine, it was time to scout out their competition. Two other trees sported "ugly" ornaments, and they were definitely creative, Team 17 admitted solemnly. But they were determined to stay positive, remembering the wise words this morning from Mrs. Rose:

"Winning is not the most important thing in a contest," she said. "There is no such thing as a contest where everyone comes in first place. You also have to know how to be a gracious non-winner. You do this by being happy for the winners and congratulating them. The important thing for this contest and for anything else you will ever do as a team is to appreciate and enjoy the experience of working together. Friendship is the real prize! Now go out there and have some fun today...and make sure you all thank the Maltbys before you leave."

"Well, the worst we can do is third place," Joel exclaimed with a grin as they viewed their competition.

"Are there second and third place prizes in this category," Mitch asked?

They didn't know.

By noon, the decorating was all done. The tree lot was a beautiful sight...well, all except for the three ugly wannabes. The others were covered with colorful and uniquely crafted popcorn ornaments and garlands. Some added gold and silver tinsel, sequins, and glittery touches to their creations. The field of decorated trees sparkled in the noonday sun.

*** 

It was time for the judging to begin. Four men walked through the crowd with notebooks in hand, carefully dodging people with cameras, including two newspaper photographers. Marty recognized "Mr. Bill," an older man who was always at the Maltby farm at Christmas time, helping people pick out trees by shaking the snow off and holding them up. The other three were strangers. They methodically analyzed each tree, then huddled together, talking briefly among themselves, finally writing in their notebooks. Their faces gave no indication of favoring any particular tree.

THE CONTEST

*Those guys are good,* Marty acknowledged silently. *I can't read their faces at all!* Reading faces was something he had learned to do very well at the orphanage. He could always tell which children were favored by potential adopters as they walked through the rec room and watched the children at play. Their eyes would always keep going back to the same one or two. He also noticed *and felt* their lack of interest as they looked him over politely but ever so briefly.

He continued to watch the judges intently as they finished with tree 17. They wrote in their notebooks and continued to tree 18.

It was finished. While the judges went into the farmhouse with Mr. Maltby to compile the list of winners, apprehension turned to chatter and laughter as kids and adults headed to the big barn for refreshments. Marty had never been in a barn before; he didn't know what to expect but was pleasantly surprised to find it so inviting. Actually, it felt like the coziest place he had ever been in! A mish-mash of different chairs, benches, and bales of hay provided comfy seats. There was a large oak table in the center filled with sandwiches, pretzels, and caramel coated popcorn balls. The smell of hot cocoa and cider mingled delightfully with the smell of hay. A friendly German Shepherd with wagging tail maneuvered its way around the barn floor, gratefully accepting whatever petting was offered. Occasionally, a few pieces of hay floated down from above, stirred up by a barn cat peering over the edge of the loft. Another cat was perched on top of a tall heater just inside the door. The heater was turned off, Marty noted, also realizing that the weather had warmed up considerably. It had turned out to be a beautiful day after such a chilly start.

An announcement from Mrs. Maltby brought everyone back outside...it was time for the awards. Excitement peaked again as they followed her to an open pavilion at the edge of the Christmas tree field. A blazing fire crackled nearby, although it certainly wasn't needed for heat. It was a bonfire that had been built while everyone was in the barn. Sticks and marshmallows for toasting were waiting on a table.

Marty, Mitch, and Joel were already familiar with the outdoor fire pit. When they were there with Mr. Rose to pick out a Christmas tree, Mr. Bill always reminded them, "Now you kids make sure you toast a few marshmallows before you leave. And help yourselves to some homemade cider." And they did! As soon as the tree was securely tied onto the top of the station wagon, they hurriedly made their way back to the tree lot for refreshments – including Mr. Rose. "I'm just a kid too," he always said. It was a perfect ending to their expedition.

Although the older Barclay kids knew the fire pit was in the pathway next to the tree lot, none of them had paid much attention to it today. They were all too busy decorating to notice it was directly in front of tree 17.

Remembering Mrs. Rose's good advice, Marty made himself a mental note: *When I thank Mr. and Mrs. Maltby for including us in their contest, I am also going to thank them for giving us a tree every year and for the cider and marshmallows. They are very nice people.*

Suddenly, Marty felt hot and sweaty, almost dizzy. Was it the cocoa, the bonfire, the afternoon sun, or just plain nervousness? He didn't know. *It must be the anticipation*, he reasoned. *But why? It's okay if we don't win. We've got Plan B...congratulate the winners, thank the Maltbys, collect our candy and go home.* He wiped his forehead and took off his heavy coat, but he was still sweaty. Then he noticed quite a few others were doing the same thing, especially those standing off to the side, closer to the bonfire – *well, all except Hannah,* he reminded himself. *She's always cold. She even wears a sweater in the rec room when the fireplace is going!*

No, even Hannah was taking her coat off! The sun was beating down; the outdoor temperature had soared. It was almost like a summer afternoon.

With cameras ready, the newspaper photographers knelt in front of the pavilion as Mr. Maltby held the list of winners in his hand. Mrs. Maltby was stationed inside the pavilion next to a pile of prizes and candy. Marty noticed two baskets sitting on the floor next to her and his excitement kicked up another notch. One was filled to overflowing with large candy canes and what looked like tins of maple sugar and boxes of ribbon candy. The other was filled with a pile of brown bags tied with rainbows of curling ribbons and three jars. He knew immediately that it *had to be* the Ugliest Popcorn Tree prize basket. He started to poke Mitch, but Mitch was also focused on the basket...*their* basket!

Mr. Maltby flashed his well-recognized, always friendly smile and thanked all the young people who took part in the contest, the adults who accompanied them, and the judges. But before he could continue, he was suddenly interrupted by what sounded like a volley of cap pistols going off.

Everyone was startled. People were turning around and looking at the bonfire. No – it wasn't the bonfire; it was just quietly burning away.

Then all eyes turned to the right – to the field of decorated trees and the sight of popcorn flying into the air and out onto the walking path. The assembly broke out in laughter as they realized the flying popcorn was coming from a tree. One of the photographers bolted to the site, followed by a contingent of curious on-lookers. The awards ceremony came to a halt as the

27

popping continued, pulling more and more of the crowd away from the pavilion.

Tree 17 was exploding!

Marty, Mitch, Hannah, and Joel rushed to their tree with all the others, jaws dropping in disbelief. The front of their tin star was shooting popcorn straight out toward the path and the people, and now the back of the star was starting to pop, shooting more out onto the back side of the tree. The manger was churning out popped corn in a steady stream, some of it blowing straight up in the air while more just popped and spilled over the side. Eyeballs were exploding everywhere, sending overheated, glue-covered popcorn and hair in all directions while the wadded-up brown paper balls were being tossed every which way. People were laughing and children were squealing with delight as they dodged the flying missiles or tried to catch them. Even Mr. and Mrs. Maltby were laughing and enjoying the unexpected attraction. Everyone was taking pictures.

"Whose tree is this?" one of the photographers shouted!

Marty, Mitch, Hanna, and Joel raised their hands ever so slightly. Now they were being lined up in front of the tree and everyone was taking pictures. Outwardly, they tried to smile, but inside they were shaking with trepidation, not knowing what to expect next.

Meanwhile, Marty noticed that the judges and Mr. and Mrs. Maltby were quickly returning to the pavilion, talking among themselves. Mr. Maltby was writing on the paper he still held in his hand. *We are being eliminated,* Marty realized. *Why else would he be writing?* He immediately felt bad for his team... his friends who had worked so hard for *this dumb decoration stuff,* and for the kids at Barclay. He tried to stay positive, but it wasn't working this time. The only positive thing he could think of was that their failed creation provided amusement for a short time. Once again, he wished he could just melt into the background and disappear, but instead, they had to go back to the pavilion and stand with the other teams!

***

Prizes were awarded first to the 5-to-7-age groups. The young Barclay team came in first in the Most Creative Popcorn Tree category. Marty, Mitch, Hannah, and Joel watched proudly as four of their own scrambled onto the pavilion floor, picked out their prizes, and, grinning from ear to ear, made their candy selection. After all the winners received their prizes, Mrs. Maltby invited the remaining 5-, 6-, and 7-year-olds to come into the pavilion for candy.

Winners in the 8-to-10 age group were announced next. There were a lot of teams in that age group. Barclay did not win, but good-naturedly cheered for the winners and stood in line to choose their candy.

It was the same scenario for the 11- and 12-year-olds...lots of teams. Barclay was not one of the winners for the most beautiful or most creative tree, of course. They did not expect to be.

The winner for The Ugliest Popcorn Tree was announced. Just as Marty suspected, they did not win. It went to the 4-H group. Amid a lot of cheers, the 4-H kids walked out of the pavilion with the huge popcorn and toppings basket. With wounded hearts, Team 17 congratulated them and followed the other 11- and 12-year-olds into the pavilion to receive their candy. Marty tried hard

– really, really hard, to switch his silent anger into positive thoughts, but he couldn't break through the wall of negativity in his mind.

*Stupid sunshine! Stupid bonfire! Stupid popcorn! Stupid decorating contest! Never again will I ever do anything dumb like this,* he promised himself. *Never again. I should have known better!*

Seconds later, they heard their names called.

"Team 17. Marty, Mitch, Hannah, and Joel, would you please come over here." It was Mr. Maltby. Almost as if being in a fog, they walked from the back of the pavilion and faced the crowd as they were asked to do while a special citation was read:

### For the Overall Most Unique Tree, a special prize is awarded to Team 17

"We know they had their tree entered in the Ugly Popcorn Tree category," he continued, "and it certainly was very well done. But in all honesty, folks, the tree was also very creative. And when it all popped out and settled down, it was also very beautiful, almost like it was covered with snow. So rather than make a determination as to where it should be, our judges decided to add a category that they felt appropriate for such unusual decorations.

Congratulations to Team 17 on The Most Unique Tree!"

The crowd erupted into cheers and applause. Team 17 couldn't believe their ears. They won a prize – a top prize! Everyone was smiling at them and taking more pictures. They shook hands with

Mr. Maltby, thanked him, and proceeded to the prize table, still in somewhat of a daze.

As they looked over the array of beautiful prizes, they conferred as a team. Each one chose something that could be used by all the kids at the orphanage: two long toboggans, a long sled, and a snow saucer. When they proceeded to the candy basket, it was empty. Mrs. Maltby handed them a very large bag of candy – enough for all the kids at the orphanage. "You can make your choices when you get back home," she said, smiling.

The trees would remain decorated for the rest of the week, to be enjoyed by other visitors to the tree farm. That made clean-up easy – they didn't have to "undecorate" until next weekend.

After enjoying some toasted marshmallows, the Barclay kids brought all of their decoration boxes, candy, and prizes to the parking lot. They loaded the van with the youngest kids first and as much else as they could fit on board for the first run back to the orphanage. The half-hour wait for Mr. Rose to return went by quickly for the remaining Barclay kids. They were joined by the German Shepherd and chatted with kids from the two scouting groups who were getting ready to leave.

As Mr. Rose was packing the van for the second run, trying to figure out the best way to transport the remaining children and cargo, one of the photographers came over and asked about the Barclay Children's Home and how he could get in touch with the person in charge. The newspaper wanted to do an article on the orphanage as well as the children who had taken part in the contest.

Two days later, a reporter and photographer arrived at Barclay to talk with Mrs. Rose.

# THE UGLY POPCORN TREE

# Barclay

They took pictures of the inside and the outside of the orphanage and a group picture of all the children but wanted to know more about the four oldest residents. Mrs. Rose invited Marty, Mitch, Hannah, and Joel to join them and answer questions themselves.

The questions were general at first, but soon became more personal. They were asked how long they had been living at the orphanage, what circumstances brought them there, and how they viewed their future.

The twins, Mitch and Hannah, told their story first. "We were six when our parents died of tuberculosis," Mitch began. "When they got to where they were real sick, they sent us to live with an aunt until they got better, but they never did. We never saw them again. Mom died first; Dad died a couple months later. Our aunt took care of us and the funerals. Then she got sick and died. We had no more family so we lived in foster homes for a while. We came to Barclay when we were nine. A year later, Hannah got adopted but I didn't. Her new family was in Philadelphia. It was a horrible feeling to have to let go of my sister, but I knew it was a good thing for her – at least I thought it was. I met her new parents and they seemed nice, plus she would have a younger brother and sister. As much as I didn't want her to go, it was supposed to be a happy time for her. I tried to think of it that way. Mrs. Rose gave us each a box of stationary and some stamps so we could write to each other. We knew it was only temporary until we grew up and could be together again. But it turned out to be a nightmare for Hannah."

The reporter looked over to Hannah. "Yes," she said quietly, "Mitch is right; it *was* a nightmare. At ten years old, and having been pretty much protected by adults and my brother, I didn't know much about having to take care of myself in the outside world. It was not a nice place at all. I was only gone for three months but they were the worst three months of my life. It was a wonderful feeling to finally come back to Barclay and everyone here, and especially to be with my brother again."

"Would you like to tell me more about the experience you had with your adoptive family, Hannah, and why you came back here?" the reporter prompted.

Hesitantly, she continued. "My main duty was to babysit my new brother and sister when I wasn't in school. They were one-and-a-half and three. When I wasn't taking care of them, I had cleaning chores – nothing I hadn't done before, nothing difficult, just a lot more than I had been used to doing. Laundry was the biggest thing, especially with two little ones and one in diapers. There was a lot of laundry so I did it every day after school.

"My parents were gone a lot. They worked different shifts and were usually very tired when they got home. They also had a lot of errands to do and meetings to go to. I didn't have to do any cooking; my parents did that, but it was my job to do the dishes and clean the kitchen afterward. Then when the children went to bed, I did my homework. Sometimes I fell asleep before it got done because I was tired, so my marks weren't very good. Then..."

The interview stopped as Hannah teared up, obviously having trouble talking. Mitch began to say something but Hannah stopped him. "I'm okay," she assured the reporter. "There are just some things I have tried to forget."

The reporter started to apologize but Hannah again assured him she was able to continue.

"Then one day my sister was sick and I had to stay home from school and take care of her so my mother could go to work. I had just fed the babies their lunch and got them put down for a nap when my father got home from his job. He was acting strange. He gave me a hug, and that was okay, although he had never hugged me before. But then...but then," Hannah hesitated again, tears welling up in her eyes.

Mitch put his hand on her arm. "Enough, Hannah?" he asked.

"No. I'm okay...really, I am. I *want* to tell this story. My father changed after that day. He kept looking at me in 'different ways' and when we were alone, he said strange things - things I didn't understand. He kept trying to hug me. One time he hugged me and wouldn't let go. I got scared and started fighting, finally getting away, and ran out of the house. I kept running but didn't have anywhere to go. I saw a good climbing tree in a back yard that was right next to a garage so I climbed the tree and got onto the garage roof and hid on the back side of it, away from the street. I saw their

35

car go by a couple of times but I hid in back of the branches and stayed real still so they wouldn't see me. Thinking about going back to that house made my almost sick to my stomach. That's when I started thinking more about <u>not</u> going back – ever...running away and getting back to Barclay somehow. But I had no money, no way to get there.

"When it got dark, I came down off the roof. I kept trying to think of where I could go, but I couldn't think of any place so I just kept walking. There were people living near the railroad tracks in tents and I asked one of the women if I could stay with her and she let me. She was real nice and she gave me a cheese sandwich. The next day she took me to the police station and told me I had to go in there and tell them my story. She said they would help me, but they didn't. Instead, they took me back home because I was reported as a runaway.

"I tried to talk to my mother, but she was very angry with me for running away. I was afraid to tell her why, afraid she wouldn't believe me and would get even madder. She told me I was just going through some homesickness for my brother and the orphanage and I had to get over it. My father didn't speak to me for quite a while. Then one day when we were alone again, he started doing the same things, hugging me real tight. He hurt me. When I cried real loud and woke my sister up, he let go. I tried to talk to my teacher but she told me I must be exaggerating. She said my parents were nice people and everybody liked them and that every child should be expected to do things around the house, including taking care of smaller children. She said that parents were supposed to hug their children and I was apparently not used to it, having lived in an orphanage. She told me I had to change my thinking if I was ever going to get used to real family life.

"I did try. Really, I did! But my father kept looking at me weird, saying things that were not nice. I tried to avoid being alone with him, but he found ways, especially when my mother was gone or sleeping. I decided that the teacher was right – I was the one who had to change because no one else was going to. But I still kept trying to find someone to talk to, someone who would listen. Then I remembered from Sunday school that God hears us no matter where we are. So I prayed real hard that He would show me a way out.

"The next day, I found a quarter on the sidewalk on my way home from school and called Mrs. Rose from a telephone booth. We only had a couple of minutes to talk and I did most of the talking. Then our time was up and we got disconnected, but I felt so much better just being able to hear her voice. I didn't know if Mrs. Rose could do anything or what was going to happen, so I still kept looking for another chance to run away – far away from that horrible house.

"Two days later, Mr. and Mrs. Rose came to the door. You can't believe how happy I was to see them! It was on a Saturday. My parents weren't home; the children were taking a nap and I was washing a load of diapers. They helped me pack while we waited for my mother. Then Mrs. Rose told me to carry my things out to the car while she and Mr. Rose talked to my mother for a few minutes. Then we left. It felt so good to be going back to Barclay and to my brother that it made me cry! But it was a happy cry. Mitch and I made a pact that we will not be separated again, and Mr. and Mrs. Rose agreed. If we are ever adopted, it will have to be by parents who are able to take both of us."

"What did you say to the mother, Mrs. Rose?" the reporter asked.

"It was a polite conversation. We did not discuss her husband. I simply reminded the mother that Hannah was not legally their child yet. There is a three-month trial period for all children who leave Barclay with prospective parents because sometimes it does not turn out to be a good match. She agreed that this was obviously not a good match."

"Have you had to reclaim other children in the past?"

"Yes."

The reporter turned back to Mitch and Hannah. "Thank you for telling me your stories. You are certainly a brave young lady, Hannah, and I think it would be good for people to know what you went through. I will need to have both of your signatures on this Permission to Print form, however, and yours also, Mrs. Rose, as their guardian."

Mitch and Hannah signed the agreement, then Mrs. Rose.

Joel was next. "I am an only child. My parents died in an automobile accident when I was eight years old. I was riding in the back seat and survived with a broken foot and a broken collar bone, but my parents died instantly I was told. I saw their bodies as I was being pulled out of the car but wish I hadn't. As much as I try to remember them as they were before the accident, that horrible picture keeps coming back into my mind, especially at night. I keep hearing the crash and the noises over and over again, especially my mother's scream. I was afraid to lay down and go to sleep for a long time. It's getting better, but I still hate going to bed."

38

Joel's eyes were misty, his voice saddened, as he hesitated briefly before continuing. "My only other relatives are an aunt and uncle who live overseas that I have never met, so I ended up in foster homes for a couple of years. I have only been here at Barclay for two years. It is the nicest place I have been so far other than my real home. Everyone has been very nice, but I still miss my parents something awful. I try to stay busy so I don't think about them as much.

"As for the future, well, maybe someday I will have new parents, but maybe not. No one seems to want an older kid, but that's okay. I'm getting used to living here. I'm just really glad there are other kids here my age."

Joel gave the reporter permission to print his story as well.

Marty's story was not as scary or traumatic, but equally compelling. "I've been here since I was about a week old. My parents didn't want me or couldn't take care of me – not sure which, but at least they left me on the porch of a good place. I am still here because I am ugly," he said matter-of-factly. "I know I am, and always will be, but that's the way God made me. I used to feel sorry for myself when I was younger and didn't understand why no one wanted me, but after a while I figured it out. People want to adopt cute children, not homely ones." Marty looked over at Mrs. Rose and gave her a closed mouth smile.

"But Mrs. Rose has encouraged me to be positive in all things," he continued, "especially being happy with myself. She told me that there is a reason why I am still here and perhaps someday I will know what that reason is. I'm thinking maybe it is to be a big brother to all the younger kids and even to some a little older like Hannah, Mitch, and Joel. Listening to them makes me realize how fortunate I am that I didn't have any bad experiences. We get to be pretty good friends here you know, but that is actually the sad part about living here...having to say goodbye to the kids who get adopted. It's like constantly losing a part of my family that I will never see again. Probably someday Mitch and Hannah and Joel will get adopted and I will be happy for them, but it will be a sad day for me when they leave.

"As for memories, I don't have any outside of Barclay; this is the only home I have ever had. Mrs. Rose keeps a scrapbook for each one of us, so I can take my memories with me when I leave. I am very thankful for Mr. and Mrs. Rose – they are kind of like parents, teachers, and friends all rolled up into two people.

"As for the future, I try to do well at school and read a lot so I can get a good job someday and be successful. Not sure what I want to be, just that I want to be very good at whatever it is. Hopefully I will be able to stay here until I am finished with school. This is a good place to live. And yes, you have permission to print my story."

***

Two prominent articles appeared on the front page of the Sunday newspaper. One was the traditional write-up and pictures of the tree decorating contest. The second was a special interest article about Barclay that included the stories of its four oldest residents.

# Families

It was a Christmas that the four "oldsters" would never forget, thanks to a popcorn contest, intentions of creating a "thing of ugly" that turned into a rather explosive portrayal of beauty, and a lot of unintended publicity. The Sunday newspaper article brought people into the orphanage from all over the area, even from neighboring Maryland and Delaware and beyond. The phone kept ringing. Barclay Children's Home and its residents were suddenly immersed in a high-profile spotlight.

Mitch and Hannah became part of a family in Maryland who already had a set of twins plus two older children, one in high school and one in college. After shuffling bedrooms and closets around, all six members of the family decided they had room in their home and hearts for two more. The other twins were two years younger than Mitch and Hannah but they meshed well in their rolls as resident twins.

Joel was adopted into a family in Pennsylvania who had lost a son several years earlier in a car accident. Like Joel, they had experienced heart-stabbing pain and a continual effort to get past the hurt. They had a lot in common. Now the grieving parents had someone to share their love with, someone to help them overcome the emptiness in their lives. But their joy was doubled. When Joel was saying goodbye to the children at Barclay, his new parents noticed a younger boy with tears running down his face and Joel quietly talking to him, wiping away the tears.

"He has been kind of a younger brother," Joel explained. "His name is Ben. I've been helping him with his school work and he usually sits next to me at dinner. I am going to miss him."

They also adopted Ben.

As for Marty, it was an emotionally tough time as he said goodbye to Mitch, Hannah, Joel, Ben, and some of the other children who got adopted as well. He was genuinely happy for all of them, but it was still sad. *So many gone all at once*, he thought as the last adopted child, a 2-year-old little girl, walked out the door with her new parents. A new kind of loneliness set in. *There's no one left here my age*, he realized, *and there probably never will be again. I'm going to be everyone's big brother from now on.* His thoughts were short-lived as they swung quickly from maturity and responsibility to loneliness and depression. He tried to think positive but, once again, it wasn't working. He knew and accepted the fact that he was not adoptable, but for the first time in his life, he resented it. He felt alone...very alone.

Then he thought about Mitch and Hannah and Joel, remembering their stories and what they had been through. He had been spared that kind of pain and felt strangely thankful for his situation. Reality, positive thinking and, most of all, his common sense returned. *No, the Roses are not my real parents. Yes, my "family" is continually changing. But what I have that the others have not had is stability. I am truly blessed!*

There. He felt better. *This is my home, and it is a wonderful place!* he acknowledged.

Mrs. Rose returned from saying goodbye to her 2-year-old girl and her adoptive parents and handed Marty three pieces of paper. He was confused at first as he scanned through them...until he realized what they were. In total disbelief and at a loss for words, he just stared at Mrs. Rose!

"I have three offers of adoption for you, Marty," she smiled. This is very unusual; you have an opportunity to choose your own parents."

"What? Three people want me?" He exclaimed. He heard the words Mrs. Rose said but they didn't seem real!

"Six people want you," she corrected. "Three sets of parents. Their names are not on these pages; I thought you should first read the section about why they want to adopt you before I give you their names. I will let you read them while I get a few of these children off to bed. I'll be back shortly, but take your time."

His stomach felt like it was full of butterflies or jumping beans or something that wouldn't sit still. He felt like he was floating through space somewhere in a make-believe world. This couldn't be happening! But it was.

He looked at the first paper: "We feel that Marty has been through a lot in his twelve years. He deserves a good home and we can do that for him. He doesn't know us, but we live just 20 miles down the road from Barclay. We have two sons – one is going into the army and the other is going off to college. It will definitely be lonely without them. Selfishly speaking, adopting another child, preferably an older boy, would fill that void in our lives. As for Marty, he would be welcomed with open arms and lots of love. Our extended family is quite large. In addition to two brothers, he would have lots of cousins."

*Wow, that would be nice,* Marty thought, finally starting to realize that this was actually about him! *I could come back here to visit from time to time. Two other children, both boys, both older. Large family. Gosh, I would have brothers older than me – big brothers! Plus cousins! I hadn't thought about cousins, aunts and uncles.*

The second was from a family in New York. "Marty is not ugly and our hearts went out to him when we read his story in the newspaper," they said. "We just had to travel to Pennsylvania to meet him, but there were others interested in him as well so we didn't have a chance to talk with him. Plus, he was preoccupied, reading the newspaper to some of the other children. We fell in love with him and would be thrilled to have him in our home. It is a busy one, but we can give him the family he has never had. We currently have twelve children – 3 biological and 9 foster. I (the mother) rode the orphan train when I was nine years old," the note continued. "I was put up on a platform in three different cities and had to recite a poem as people looked me over. It was a horrible experience being examined like cattle along the way. I ended up in Nebraska but ran away after a few years and got back to the familiar streets of New York. I eventually made a good life here. One of my biggest goals in adulthood is to provide a loving home for as many orphaned children or children in distress as I can. I know how they feel. My husband agrees and feels the same way."

*New York! How did they find out about Barclay? How did our newspaper get all the way up there? They traveled all this way to see me? Why? What's an orphan train?* There was a picture attached of a very large house and a group of children next to a pool. *Looks like a smaller version of Barclay except for the pool and the porch,* he thought. *It would probably feel like home rather quickly.*

He picked up the third paper. The explanation was shorter than the others: "Marty is the beautiful child we have always wanted, wished for, but not blessed with, although we were parents for a very short time. We know Marty – not well, but well enough to know he is beautiful inside and out. He has a caring heart. We cannot offer him a family with sisters or brothers as we have no children. All we can offer him is our home and our love. We pray that he will adopt us."

*They <u>know</u> me? Who are they? <u>How</u> do they know me?*

Marty was full of questions by the time Mrs. Rose returned. "Mrs. Rose, who are these people? When were they here? I don't remember anyone looking at me or talking to me. What's an orphan train?"

"Oh, they were here alright. Well, at least four of the parents were – the ones who had never met you. You didn't pay much attention to them - as usual." Mrs. Rose smiled as she emphasized "as usual." "You gave them a quick glance as they walked through, but they spent quite a bit of time watching you while you were reading the newspaper to some of the other kids. I told them you were an avid reader and, besides the newspaper, you read books to the little ones every night before they go to bed.

"As for orphan trains, they are a thing of the past," Mrs. Rose explained. "For seventy or eighty years, thousands of children who were orphaned for whatever reasons and living on streets up and down the East Coast were dressed up real nice, put on trains, and taken out west. There were a lot of families out there who wanted and needed children, especially farm families. Sometimes it was a good thing and sometimes it wasn't. The trains stopped in 1929. I know all this because Mr. Rose was an orphan train child. His parents died a few years apart and he and his younger brother had nowhere to live except the street. They were put on one of those trains and adopted by a family in Kansas. They were fortunate enough to both be taken in by the same family. It worked out well, but he missed Pennsylvania. When he grew up, he decided to come back here to live but his brother didn't remember much about Pennsylvania and stayed with his Kansas family. I'm glad he came back here because this is where we met. Someday you will have to ask Mr. Rose about riding on the orphan train when he was eight years old. It's a very interesting story. The one lady who wants to adopt you and was an orphan train rider probably has an interesting story of her own."

"Wow. So, if I lived back then, I probably would have been on one of those trains?"

"Maybe. It would have depended on whether you were in a foster home or an orphanage or living on the street. They usually took the street kids first. When Mr. Rose was orphaned, there weren't many sanctioned orphanages and the foster homes were pretty full. At least he was old enough to care for himself and his brother, even though they didn't have a real place to live. They moved into an alley with a lot of other boys who kind of camped together until one day they were all rounded up, given baths and clean clothes, put on a train, and moved out west."

"Well, I guess then I should be thankful I was born when I was and not back then. Even though my parents didn't want me or couldn't take care of me, at least they left me on the porch of a good place and you took me in. Someday, though," he added pensively, "I would like to hear about Mr. Rose's trip on the orphan train."

Mrs. Rose smiled at the boy whom she had raised for all of his twelve years. It was a bittersweet moment as the memory of his arrival played through her mind once again. She and her husband had no children of their own; Marty was as close to being their son as any child could be. They talked about legally adopting him at one time but reluctantly deciding against it, realizing that it would not be in Marty's best interest. By not adopting him, he would have a chance to become part of a normal family, perhaps even with brothers and sisters. But it never happened.

Now the time was here – the time they were going to have to let him go. It was exciting but sad. They hoped with all their hearts that whatever he chose to do would prove to be a good decision and that he would be happy.

"Mrs. Rose, who is the couple who said they know me? Are they from church or my school?"

"No, they are not from church or your school, and they have never been here, at least not yet. They were afraid that if you saw them, you would wonder why they were here as they would have no reason to be. They felt that if they talked with you as prospective parents, you'd think they were feeling sorry for you, and they didn't want that either. They said you are a caring, energetic young man and one to be admired for all the things you do for others. Here are the first pages with names and more information. I will give you time to read them by yourself while I take care of a couple chores."

\*\*\*

Never had Marty felt such anxiety. His future was in his hands! He was actually going to be leaving Barclay and going to live with one of these people! Strangely enough, he didn't feel ready. Less than an hour ago, he was feeling rejected because he *wasn't* leaving like some of the other kids were. Now he *was* going to be leaving and didn't know if he wanted to. A strange feeling of homesickness washed over him. Just the thought of leaving....

Without looking at the papers, he set them on the table next to him and looked around the rec room where he had spent so much of his life. He knew every inch of it; it was filled with twelve years of memories.

The Christmas tree was still decorated, sitting peacefully in the corner, covered with homemade decorations and tinsel. As always, there were a few on the floor. Barnie was stretched out in front of the fireplace of dying embers, enjoying the last bit of warmth. There was just something peaceful about sitting alone with the Christmas tree and fireplace. He did it every year. It was a time for reflection – a time for remembering those who had left.

But now it was his turn, and it was real! He pulled himself back into the moment, picked up the papers, and scanned for names and locations, matching them with the descriptions he had read.

He didn't recognize the names of the couple who lived 20 miles down the road. The New York couple lived in Albany.

With curiosity at a peak, he flipped to the last page...and sat up with a start. It was signed by William and Maria Maltby!

*The Maltbys want to adopt me? This can't be true! Why?* He searched for the matching page and read their statements again. *They know me and think I am a beautiful child?!*

Marty's head was still spinning when Mrs. Rose returned once again. She knew by the look on his face that he read the names and what was surely on his mind...the Maltbys. Taking a seat across from him, she looked deeply into his face.

"Marty, tell me how you feel. What are you thinking?"

"I don't know, Mrs. Rose. This whole thing is unbelievable. All these people actually wanting me sounds too good to be true, but...the Maltbys? They want to adopt me? Or, as they say, they want me to adopt them? They would be my first choice, of course. I know them and I wouldn't have to move far away. But what if it doesn't work out? Would we still be friends? If they decided after a while that I was a mistake, would they...." His voice trailed off. "I know they are nice people, but...."

Mrs. Rose smiled warmly. "There is no guarantee with the Maltbys, Marty, or with either of the other families. But whichever one you choose, if it is not a good fit, you know you can always come back here. I can tell you a little bit more about the Maltbys if it will help you."

"Yes, I would like to know more."

"I learned that the Maltbys had a son a long time ago, but he only lived for a few days. That is why they said they were parents for a very short time. Maria Maltby almost died, too, and it was a quite a while before she recuperated, physically and mentally. It was when William was overseas in the army. He wasn't able to be home when their child was born, not only because he was in combat, but because he was wounded and almost died himself. He had actually been reported as killed in combat but later it was determined to be a mistake. Unfortunately, the false report about William plus the loss of her child, both at the same time, pulled Maria into a state of devastation. When it was discovered that William was alive and returned home, it was a happy occasion, of course, but they still went through a few rough years. As you know, they have done a lot of nice things for the children in the community for a long time, but it might have had something to do with their own need for healing."

Marty had never thought much about Mr. and Mrs. Maltby as regular people – they were the owners of a tree farm. But right now, they were becoming very real.

Mrs. Rose knew that Marty was feeling overwhelmed. She appreciated that he was a common sense, look-at-the-facts-and-figure-it-out young person. He needed to be alone.

"Why don't you take time to think about all of this, Marty," Mrs. Rose suggested. "There is no hurry. Let me know when you decide what you want to do or if you would like to talk some more. I'll see you in the morning."

He added a few logs to the fire and stayed in the rec room, knowing there was no way he was going to sleep if he went to bed.

Besides, watching the flames in the otherwise darkened room would help him think. He smiled as Barnie yawned and stretched on his rug, obviously enjoying the additional heat. The years of living at Barclay played through his mind like movie clips. Again, he saw the faces of so many kids who had come and gone, imagining where they were now and wondering if they were happy. A mix of memories, emotions, and questions flooded his mind.

*Do I really want to leave Barclay*, he pondered? *Yes and no*, he answered himself truthfully. *Am I afraid to leave? Again, yes and no. If I stay until I finish school, what will happen to me then? Where will I go as an adult? I still won't have a family; I will have passed up that opportunity. Will I regret it? Probably. So, I need to make a decision. If I had to go home with one family right now, which one would I choose? Maltbys. Why? Because I know them and I would be able to live in the area I am familiar with. Are those good reasons? I don't know. Could I be just as happy someplace else? Probably.*

He forced himself to imagine life with the family 20 miles away and then with the family in Albany. He pictured the parents, siblings, schools, and his future. He mentally reviewed and rereviewed all of his options and how he felt about each one.

Suddenly, someone was gently shaking him. "Good morning, Marty." It was Mr. Rose. "If you would like more time to yourself or more time to sleep, you can go into our room. It's going to be getting a little noisy down here in a few minutes," he added with a smile.

Marty blinked at the sunlight coming through the windows. It was morning! He could already hear the footsteps of children coming down the stairs and the rising level of chatter. Barnie was outside, barking to come in.

"No thanks, Mr. Rose. I know what I am going to do."

The usual day's activities were well underway when Marty and Mr. and Mrs. Rose were able to be alone at the kitchen table.

"I've decided on Mr. and Mrs. Maltby," Marty announced…not only because I know them, but because I want to get to know them better. I want to adopt them," he grinned.

# *A New Life*

Marty L. Smith was now Marty William Maltby. The adoption papers were signed at the courthouse the second week in January with the usual three-month waiting period for finalization. Mr. and Mrs. Rose and Mr. Bill, the Maltby's helper, were on hand to add their signatures as witnesses. Afterward, they all celebrated with lunch at a downtown diner that Marty had walked by many times but had never been in. *The Maltbys sure know a lot of people,* Marty concluded as he continued to receive shake hands and hugs from the diner patrons. Everyone was congratulating the Maltbys and welcoming Marty as he was introduced as their new son. Never had he felt so special...so "included."

***

It was strange that first day, being on the tree farm and not anticipating going back to Barclay...even stranger to actually be inside the Maltby home. His bedroom was upstairs with a panoramic view of the farm. He looked out over acres of neatly planted rows of trees, natural wooded areas, a creek that wound its way through one corner of the farm, and distant rolling hills – so different from the sidewalks and buildings of town.

All of his personal belongings were sitting on the bed, waiting to be put away, although his new mom and Mrs. Rose had already hung up all of his clothes. There was a cork bulletin board on the wall next to his bed with a picture tacked right in the middle – a group picture of all the kids from Barclay and signatures of those who were old enough to write. It was a picture that Mrs. Rose took right after Christmas when so many of the kids were getting ready to leave. Marty was standing in the back row with Mitch, Hannah and Joel. It didn't make him homesick; it made him feel good to know that many of those kids were also settling into new lives and becoming part of their adoptive families.

He smiled at a set of shelves on another wall with a collection of miniature tractors taking up the whole top shelf. Somehow, he knew they were from his new dad! No, he didn't know any more about tractors or farm life than he did about family life, but he had a feeling he was going to like all of it – especially with the smell of whatever his mom was cooking downstairs!

***

It didn't take long for Marty to fit comfortably into his new role as the Maltby son. He and Choco, the friendly German shepherd, quickly became good friends, especially when Marty volunteered to brush him, just like he used to do with Barnie back at the orphanage. He only did it a few times before Choco caught on and automatically plopped the brush at his feet every morning after breakfast. Wherever Marty was, Choco was nearby – well, until a car pulled into the driveway or until people started arriving for an event or business. Then Choco left to assume his job as official greeter.

The farm was not only beautiful, it was busy. There were always things to do, although Marty didn't have any assigned duties other than brushing Choco. Instead, he and his dad consulted each evening on plans for the next day. They started with the calendar, who was coming over, and what they wanted to discuss. "It's important to make people feel important, son," his dad said. "Whether they are customers or friends or both, we want them to feel welcome here, just like we would want to feel if we visited them."

Visiting was something new to Marty. Except for his daily trip to retrieve the newspaper from Schultz's Barber Shop, he never went visiting when he lived at Barclay. It was different here; interfacing with people was important. He was kind of shy at first, mostly listening rather than talking, as he didn't know many people. But the more he learned about the farm, the trees, and the gift shop, the more he became part of the conversation. One man even referred to him as "Young Maltby," indicating that if William Maltby wasn't available, one could talk to Young Maltby!

Then there was a separate list of things that "should be done." As spring got closer, there were more of those kinds of chores, such as heeling in new trees while the ground was soft and trimming certain varieties of trees before the new growth appeared. Sometimes his mom joined them, although Marty had a feeling she was thankful that his dad had a helper so she could spend more time in the house and in her kitchen garden.

Marty never appreciated how beautiful spring was until it arrived on the farm. Many of the saplings were sprouting flowers and leaves. Daffodils and crocus blooms were everywhere. A multitude of birds were building nests in the larger trees and around the porch, being closely watched by a new family of barn cats. He became "attuned" to the sounds of nature...those that were normal and those that were not normal.

But more than anything else, for the first time in his life, he felt a true sense of belonging – a feeling of permanence. He was so caught up in learning new things that he even forgot about being homely! It didn't matter here. He was totally loved, accepted, and appreciated for who he was and whatever he did. He even smiled a lot more – crooked teeth and all! He loved his new parents, his new home, and his new life!

# Life Changes Again

It happened on a Monday in mid-April when school was not in session for a couple of days. Marty was in the big barn, sweeping up some of the hay that was spread around the floor after a Boy Scout outing over the weekend. He was never in "Scouts," but recognized a couple of the boys from school. The gathering gave him a chance to actually see and experience some of their activities. After he helped them build a bonfire, they invited him to stay for the evening, listen to stories, sing songs, and toast marshmallows. It was a really fun time and Marty got to hear about some of the good things that they did. Yes, it seemed like something he would like to do, and his parents agreed.

But there was something even more important on his mind this morning. He was waiting for his dad to swing by on the tractor and pick him up. They were going out to a newly-turned field to plant saplings – and Marty was going to drive! He could hardly believe his ears after they made their plans last night and his dad said, "Want to drive tomorrow?" At first, he was stunned. Yes! was his emphatic reply. He had been paying very close attention to all the things his dad did when they were riding around, and now he was excited with the thought of learning how to drive! After all, he was almost 13!

57

As he swept the straw into a somewhat neat pile, he remembered the first time he was in the big barn just months ago, enjoying cocoa and pretzels and waiting for the awards to be announced for the tree decorating contest. He smiled as he recalled how his life changed several times that day. He thought about all the work Team 17 put into making their popcorn tree ugly and the anticipation of winning a coveted prize. Then there was the agonizing disaster when their tree decided to follow its own path to beauty instead of remaining ugly, causing them to lose the contest. The emotional roller coaster continued into sheer delight when they won a prize after all – in a category that hadn't even existed when the contest started. Then they transitioned from being nobodies to front-page prominence. He, Mitch, Hannah and Joel went from being over-the-hill orphans to being adopted into families. What a whirlwind of activity that day started – and all because of an ugly popcorn tree!

A playful barn kitten attacked his broom as it went by, swatting at it a few times and then jumping back, returning Marty to the present. He laughed and gave the little intruder a friendly boost out of the way. Choco was lying next to a hay bale, patiently allowing his tail to be ambushed by two of the other kittens...until a horn honked. That meant someone was in the driveway. Choco was off and running. Marty leaned his broom against the wall and followed. As he rounded the corner, Mr. Rose was emerging from the Barclay station wagon.

"Hi, Marty. How goes it? Are you behaving or misbehavin," he said with a chuckle?

"Hopefully I am behaving, Mr. Rose, but you'd better ask my parents to be sure," he replied with a grin. "Is everything good at Barclay?"

"Yes it is. I'm just delivering this scrapbook to you and your mom and dad. We had to get a lot of rolls of film developed after you and all your buddies left at Christmas, you know. Mrs. Rose just finished bringing all the books up to date and I'm heading to the post office to send them off. You're getting a special delivery," he added warmly. "Are your parents home?"

Before Marty could answer, he heard his mother's cheerful voice on the other side of the screen door. "Come on in, Jake Rose. Have you had breakfast? I've still got some biscuits and fried apples in the kitchen. A fresh pot of coffee won't take but a few minutes."

Jake Rose didn't need a second invitation. The sound of an approaching tractor told them that William Maltby was going to be close behind. They all sat around the kitchen table, chatting like real home folks. Marty glanced at the newest pictures in his scrapbook and handed it to his mother, intending to spend more time looking at them later. Right now, he was more anxious to find out about Mitch, Hannah and Joel.

"They're doing fine, as far as we know," was Mr. Rose's reply. "We got a letter from Hannah a few days ago and it sounds like she and Mitch are keeping busy with their schoolwork. They've had some catching up to do because their new school is a little ahead of the one they were in back here. Their family is planning a weekend in Ocean City next month and Hannah is talking about taking flute lessons over the summer. Apparently, music education is part of the curriculum for where they are in Maryland. Mitch is thinking about saxophone or drums. They sound happy. Haven't heard from Joel yet, but boys aren't usually much for writing letters."

Meanwhile, Maria Maltby was casually leafing through the scrapbook, enjoying the pictures of her new son and the collection of his early art work as she sipped her coffee. Suddenly her cup clattered noisily onto its saucer. Her eyes were wide, unmoving, fixed on the last page.

"That's the picture of Marty the night we brought him in from the porch," Jake Rose explained almost apologetically as he looked over her shoulder, "and there's the note that was in the crate with him. Didn't my wife tell you that was how we found him?" he asked with a puzzled look."

"Yes, she did, Jake. It's just that…"

"What's the matter, Maria?" William asked his wife. "Why are you looking so startled?"

Marty was just as surprised as the others, not knowing what was so obviously upsetting his mother. Slightly bewildered, he sat quietly. It seemed like an eternity before she answered.

"That blanket! Marty is wrapped in a blanket that was made by my sister! It's a pattern she created herself. No one but Ophelia crocheted a baby blanket with a giraffe like that. She only made it for special people because it took a lot of time to work in the different colors of yarn for the spots on the giraffe. Ophelia must have known Marty's birth mother! She must have known her *very well.*"

Marty looked at his dad, still confused, as William Maltby offered an explanation: "Aunt Ophelia died quite a few years ago, Marty. She lived just down the road from here. Her husband died a few years before she did. They never had any children of their own but always loved kids. She was a wonderful woman and a great comfort to your mother when I was in the army. I don't know what we would have done without her, especially after...."

His voice dropped; his eyes became misty. But Maria Maltby didn't notice; she was still staring at the picture.

Jake Rose stood up. "Well, all you folks - I need to get along to the post office. Stop by or give a call if you want to talk to Elizabeth about what's in that book, Maria. She will remember more than I do. She might even still have that blanket tucked away somewhere. Not sure, but she might. I appreciate the coffee and biscuits."

As soon as goodbyes were said and Jake Rose drove out of the driveway, Maria Maltby returned to the kitchen table. She picked up the scrapbook and looked at the picture again. Planting trees and driving the tractor were sidetracked. The conversation was obviously going to continue.

Marty was uneasy about what he should do, if anything, but felt compelled to tell what he already knew: "Mrs. Rose told me about your son that died when Dad was overseas, Mom. She told me how you almost died, too, and so did Dad. I am sorry that you had all that pain." He didn't know what else to say, so he returned to just sitting quietly, waiting for his mother to say something...anything!

"Maria." Mr. Maltby urged. "That was a long time ago. What difference does it make if Ophelia knew Marty's mother? It makes sense that she probably lived around here. Otherwise, why would she have left Marty at the orphanage? You are making Marty and me uncomfortable."

"I'm sorry," was the quiet response that finally came. With a tear rolling down her cheek, she looked up at her husband. "But do you realize that if Ophelia knew Marty's birth mother well enough to make one of these blankets for her, his mother must have been around here for a long time. She might still be here! She may have read all that stuff in the newspaper. I just don't want her to appear at our door someday and tell us she wants Marty back." What would we do? What could we do?" There were more tears as she looked imploringly at her husband.

Marty's response was from his heart and instantaneous. "Mom, please don't cry," he consoled as he rushed to kneel on one knee in front of her. "I'm not going anywhere. I really don't care who my real mother and father were or are; they didn't want me; they gave me away. You *wanted* me and I have never been happier in my whole life than I am right now. We are a family – legally. We signed the final papers Friday. No one can separate us! Please don't cry."

Her smile slowly returned. She dried her tears, hugged her son, and relaxed. Choco nuzzled his way into the middle of the group, knowing there was something wrong with his humans and they surely must need his attention.

"Well, you two had better get those trees planted before you lose the best part of the day," she said in response to her relieved but still worried-looking husband and son. "I am going to be fine. That was just a big shock for me. Right now, I need some quiet time to remind myself how blessed we are and to stop thinking about things that might happen but probably never will."

They all agreed. They were family and that's the way it was going to stay. No one was going to change it!

"Come on, Marty. You've got a date with a tractor," his dad reminded him good-naturedly. "Let's get you behind the wheel!"

***

It was a good day, despite its emotional start. With Dad at his side, Marty made several laps around the farm with the tractor, pulling a small, homemade trailer behind, loaded with tools and saplings. After he got used to the feel of the steering wheel and the sound of the gears, he practiced backing up, making the trailer go the way he wanted it to go. Then he learned how to hook and unhook the trailer without any help.

They planted trees for a couple of hours and decided to call it a day. Marty drove the tractor back to the shed and parked with no effort at all. What a sense of accomplishment! What a day it had been! A bountiful meal, a hot shower, and Marty was ready for bed! But the events of the day floated through his mind again and again. He couldn't sleep.

*Could my real parents still live around here? Why DID they give me away? If they do live around here, have they ever thought about* *me? Have they ever walked or driven by the orphanage and wondered how I was doing? Did they ever see me when I was growing up? Would they even recognize me? Did they <u>ever</u> care about me?* Then he thought about Aunt Ophelia and had a chilling thought. *If Aunt Ophelia knew my real mother, which she apparently did, there is probably a good chance that Mom...my <u>new</u> mom, knew my mother too.*

As he looked at the tired eyes of his parents the next morning, he realized that he wasn't the only one who didn't get much sleep. He wasn't surprised when, after breakfast, his dad suggested they all go into the parlor for a family meeting.

"Marty, your mother and I talked a little after you want to bed last night and feel that this might be a good time to fill you in on some family history, especially since you already know part of it from Mrs. Rose. We'd like to tell you more about the son we only had for a short time, the war years, and maybe answer any questions you might have. That is, if you want to know."

"Sure, dad. I do want to know. I care."

"Well, we were given this chunk of land by my parents as a wedding gift. I grew up in that old farm house next door and this was part of my family property. The thinking was that I would farm it just like my dad and my grandfather did but, in all honesty, by the time your mom and I got married, I was tired of farming...at least in the traditional sense. I was tired of trying to grow crops that depended on rain and sunshine and fertilizer and sweat and long days, only to lose so much of it when we had a drought or too much rain. I just didn't want that kind of life for my wife and family. What

I really wanted were horses – my own plus maybe a stable for boarding other people's horses.

"My second plan was for a veterinarian business with kennels for boarding cats and dogs and open areas for them to run. I wanted something that had to do with animals instead of crops, something that didn't depend on the growing season or the weather. Your mother understood and shared that dream with me. She actually came up with the idea of a tree farm to start with…something that was a one-time effort and didn't require constant care; something that would be successful despite the weather and would give us an income while we were developing our animal businesses. So that's what we did. We spent our first five years of marriage clearing land and planting trees. Then we built the big barn. You might have noticed that it is partitioned off in sections at the far end. Those were going to be horse stalls.

"But in 1941, before we could buy a single horse, our country was attacked when the Japanese bombed Pearl Harbor. It was just a few weeks before Christmas. The war had been going on for quite a while over in Europe but bombing Pearl Harbor and killing thousands of our military brought it home to the United States. Our whole country changed after that. A lot of men I knew joined the army, and I did, too. It took me a few months to get everything squared away here at home first, but Maria assured me that she could handle the tree farm while I was gone. It was a tough decision, especially since we were expecting our first child, but we both felt it was the right thing to do…helping to protect our country, that is.

"The house and farm didn't need a lot of tending to when I left, so your mom got a job down at the factory making parts for army vehicles, along with a crew of other women. Every day, she saw exhausted mothers leaving the factory at the end of their shift and going home to kids who, out of necessity, had been left alone. It was a tough time for women and children, trying to keep things going at home while they were worrying about the men folk.

"Then someone got the idea of converting an empty warehouse into a meeting place for school-age boys and girls. It would be a place where they could go and be together after school, have something to eat, do their homework, and enjoy crafts and activities – a place to take their minds off missing their fathers as well as their busy mothers. Your mom was a big part of that effort. After it was built, she worked there as a volunteer when she got out of her factory job in the afternoon. It was only a few hours a day, but she loved working with the young people. She even helped them collect scrap metal and tires for the war effort and paraded through town with them as they deposited their stash at the recycling plant.

"The bottom line was: she wore herself out." He looked away from his son and glanced over at Maria, who sat quietly and without expression.

"Then just before the baby was due to be born," he continued, "things went haywire. She got a telegram from the army saying I had been killed in combat. It turned out to be a mistake, but she didn't know it at the time. What really happened was I got shot through the shoulder and neck. When the medics found me, I was unconscious but still alive, lying in a field with dozens of dead G.I.s; my I.D. tag had been shot off. I don't remember being found or transported – nothing until I woke up in a hospital tent, unable to speak or move. I was paralyzed. It was months before my spine healed enough that I could move my hand to write and I started to talk again.

In the meantime, however, telegrams got sent to the families of the dead soldiers, identified by their I.D. tags, informing them of the death of their family member. My I.D. tag was separated from my body, but in the confusion of war, it triggered one of those letters." William stopped and turned to his wife. "Maria, would you like to take over and tell Marty what went on with you?"

Marty was entranced by the story as he looked from his father to his mother. They both seemed so tired. Maybe it was from lack of sleep, but he also sensed they were reliving memories from a time of sadness in their lives, memories they didn't talk about much. Maybe it was a combination of both. He didn't know, but his heart was aching for them.

"The telegram from the army was devastating, of course," Maria Maltby began. "I *was* exhausted and this was another blow to my physical health. I couldn't imagine life without him. The only thing that kept me going and sane was knowing that I was going to have a child – *our* precious child. But just before the baby was born, I became ill – feverish, probably a flu or something. Ophelia was here day and night taking care of me, bless her heart. I apparently drifted in and out of lucidness as the illness took hold. I vaguely remembered her telling me that I had a son but she didn't want me to hold him until I was better in case I was contagious. She was always the sensible one. She showed him to me from a few feet away. He was beautiful."

Maria's voice was getting raspy. She stopped. Marty and his dad knew she was recalling deep emotions, but there was nothing they could say or do until she decided to continue...or not. She cleared her throat and sat up straight in her chair. "Then I was told my child died. It was the day my world totally crashed! I remember the tears in Ophelia's eyes when she broke the news to me. He had developed a breathing problem, she said. The doctor tried to save him, but nothing worked and...and he died! I knew right then it was all my fault! I should have known better than to let myself get run down. I should have been smart enough to take better care of myself for my baby's sake, but it was too late. Then I collapsed into a depression, apparently something that happens when a person has to escape from reality." There was another pause; her face reflecting painful memories.

William moved over and sat on the sofa next to his wife with a comforting arm around her shoulder. "I'm sorry, William, Marty," she apologized. "I didn't mean to put a damper on this beautiful day, but..."

"Maybe that's enough for a while, Maria," William suggested, hugging her shoulders.

"No," she insisted with a new resoluteness. "I...we need to talk about this once in a while. It hurts, but it also helps the hurt, if that makes any sense."

Marty got up and moved to the other side of his mom. He didn't know why – it just felt good to be closer.

"I don't remember much of anything until my illness passed," she continued, staring out into the emptiness of the room in front of her. "I do know that Ophelia was with me the whole time, which was probably several more days, until I finally decided to join the rest of the world. She was so wonderful, Ophelia was, in spite of the fact that she was dealing with her own severe illness. She had muscular dystrophy and it was definitely taking its toll on her, but she put her own problems aside and took care of me. She even saw to it that the baby received a proper burial. He lies in a little grave site in front of the oak tree at the edge of the farm. Our friend Bill dug it for her. He said that Ophelia personally helped him lower the box into the ground, although he had to help her get up off her knees afterward. She said a beautiful prayer for the baby, he told me; she felt it was her duty to make sure our child was buried proper-like with the right words said over his coffin.

"Three months later, I received a second telegram from the army telling me that William was not dead; he was on his way home with a medical discharge. I will never forget that day. The news was like a ray of sunshine in a storm. But it was late in the day, too late to go to the hospital to visit Ophelia and share the good news. Her illness had overcome her and she was in the hospital. I had been with her most of the day so I decided to wait and see her the next morning. But she went into a coma overnight and died just before I got there. It was another devastating blow. I wish I would have tried harder to see her the night before; I know the news about William would have given her happiness, maybe put her mind at rest a little.

"The next days were filled with Ophelia's funeral. As her only living relative, I saw to her burial and took care of her affairs.

"It was definitely a sad year, but having my husband back home was an unexpected miracle. Together, and with time, we learned to appreciate God's timing rather than ours, to stop asking 'why' when bad things happened to us, and to be thankful for all the blessings He has given us. Now we have you," his mother smiled, "and you bless us every day."

Marty could feel his own throat starting to choke up, but his dad chimed in with a new positiveness in his voice: "Yes! Now we finally have the son we always wanted, and you are very special to both of us, Marty. And as you said earlier, we also have never been happier than we are right now because you have brought sunshine into our lives.

"And speaking of sunshine," he added with an especially big, mischievous grin, "I've been meaning to tell you about that Ugliest Popcorn Tree contest. Your team really did win – that is until your tree decided to make a grand exit by popping itself right out of the ugly category. Your mother and I and the judges had all of five minutes to come up a solution while everyone was diverted. We bumped the second place up to first and created a whole new category just for your team. We were almost as creative as you guys were," he added with a laugh, "but with a whole lot less time! Your team really did do a good job. I personally liked the bloodshot eyes with the multi-colored eyebrows!"

That elicited a hearty laugh, especially from Marty. The hairy eyebrows were his idea!

Maria Maltby surprised them with a new request. "There is a chest upstairs in the attic that is full of baby clothes and toys," she said. "Could you bring it down for me before you leave? I know all that stuff is many years old, but I'm thinking that Mrs. Rose might be able to use some of it for the toddlers at Barclay. Then I can toss the rest of it away. It is time to put it to good use or let it go. Today is the day!"

Marty and his dad pulled the trunk down the attic stairs, dusted it off, and set it in front of Maria. She opened it up to reveal a sea of pastel knitted and crocheted baby clothes, rattles, toys, blankets, an unopened baby book, and a bundle of diapers. "Well, this should keep me busy until you two get back from town," she said as she started to poke through the contents.

Town? "Omigosh, Dad, that's right – we were going to go to that tractor auction this morning! You wanted to bid on that old Chalmers™."

William Maltby laughed. "Well, if we missed it, I'll buy you a root beer float with the money we saved!" They headed out the door.

"Choco's going with us," Marty called back to his mother.

***

The one thing in particular that Maria was looking for in the trunk was not there...the giraffe blanket Ophelia made that would have been exactly like the one Marty was wrapped in when he was delivered to the orphanage. It wasn't a sad thing; she just wanted to show him what it looked like – the intricate design and how her sister wound and wove all the different colors together to create her special blankets. It should have been in there, but it wasn't. Puzzled, she stared into the empty trunk, trying to remember what else she possibly would have done with it.

*Maybe I kept it out because Ophelia made it and I didn't want to store it away. Yes, that's probably what I would have done so she wouldn't think I was inconsiderate of her time and work. Maybe it's tucked away in the upstairs closet.*

71

A thorough search of the upstairs closet brought her up empty-handed. From the kitchen to the attic, she looked every place she could think of – drawers, closets, boxes, trunks that she hadn't opened for a long time, finally coming to the conclusion that it was gone. *What would I possibly have done with it,* she wondered?

William and Marty came home to a pensive Maria. "William, that blanket that Ophelia made for me…the giraffe blanket, was not in the trunk you brought down. I wanted to show it to Marty, and I've looked everywhere it could possibly be in this house, but it's not here! I never would have given it away; it should be here."

William shrugged. "I wasn't around when all this stuff was packed away, dear, so I can't shed any light on it. The baby stuff was gone when I got home. Do you remember actually putting it in the trunk?"

"Let me think." She put her head back on the chair, closed her eyes, and allowed her mind to take her back to that time and the memories she had purposely tried to block out for years. "No. I remember handing all the baby things to Ophelia to take up to the attic and put in the trunk because I didn't have the energy to go up and down those stairs. But I don't remember giving her the blanket. I probably would not have done that – given it to her so she could pack that precious blanket away. Even in a distraught state of mind, I would not have hurt her feelings. I must have kept it out, but where would I have put it?"

"Maybe she took it back and gave it to someone else," William suggested. "You said it took a lot of time and effort to make one of those things, so maybe knowing you were packing all the baby things away, she decided to take it back. You can't blame her if she did; it would have been a sensible thing to do and Ophelia *was* sensible."

Marty had remained silent through the entire blanket conversation, just listening. But bits and pieces of a strange puzzle were trying to come together in his mind, and they were scaring him! He was starting to see a picture that, in one way, didn't make sense...but in another way, it did! He tried to push it away, telling himself that there couldn't possibly be a connection, *but he wanted to know! He had to know!* He had to know the answers to two questions before he could erase it from his mind. He proceeded cautiously.

"Mom, what was the date your son was born?"

"June 29th, 1942. Why, Marty?"

"Just wondering. Um, one more question. When was the last time you remember *actually seeing the blanket?* Is it possible your son was buried with it?"

Maria had to stop and really ponder that question. "No, he wasn't. I'm sure he wasn't. He was three days old when he died and was buried a day or two later. I was still feverish, but I do remember Ophelia saying she dressed him in his white baptismal outfit and matching white blanket, which was very thoughtful. Everything else was still in his room and his bureau. The giraffe blanket was laying over the end of his crib. That's where I put it. Funny, though. I know my mind was still groggy when we packed everything away, but I don't remember folding it up or giving it to Ophelia to put into storage. It seems like I would have at least offered to let her have it back. All I remember is that she was determined to put all that stuff away for me, knowing I couldn't go up and down the attic stairs very well and her own legs were getting weaker. She wore braces on her legs most of the time but she had to take them off to go up the attic stairs. Getting all that stuff put away was a kind thing to do for me while she still could."

William looked intently at Marty, noticing his hesitancy to speak. "What are you thinking, son? Are we overlooking something that you thought of?"

This was it! He either had to speak or remain silent; he felt a chill as he wavered, trying to decide.

"Marty? I sense you have something on your mind," his dad prodded. "Please tell us."

"I...I really don't know how to say what I am thinking and I don't want you to think I am goofy, so please forgive me if I am speaking when I shouldn't be. But there is another piece of information that kind of fits into this time frame and what you are saying. But it might not have anything to do with your son at all. Maybe it's just about a blanket."

He swallowed hard and once again blurted out what he was thinking: "Your son was born on June 29th, 1942 and died three days later. That would have been July 1st, maybe the 2nd. I was left on the front porch of the orphanage on July 3rd, 1942. They estimated I was about a week old. I was wrapped in one of your sister's blankets."

A dead silence followed as William and Maria Maltby grappled with the significance of what he was saying. "Marty, are you suggesting that you...that Ophelia...."

"I don't know, Mom. I only know from what you have said that she was a wonderful, caring person, but it just seems very strange that these things were all happening at the same time. It's probably all coincidence, but it still seems weird."

Silence filled the room again; no one knew what to say. Marty stood so still he could hardly breathe, not knowing what effect his words would have on his parents. William broke the stillness.

"There's one sure way to solve this mystery. Maria, do you have an objection to my calling Bill and having him show me exactly where the grave is that he dug for Ophelia? I think we should open it."

Maria was startled, but only for a few seconds. "No, I have no objection. I want to know also...but I don't want to be there."

"I'll be back in a little while." He started for the door and then turned around. "Marty, do you want to come with me or do you want to stay here with your mother?"

Marty looked over at his mother.

"Go ahead, son. Go with your dad and Bill if you care to. I will wait here."

# THE UGLY POPCORN TREE

# The Truth

Shovels in hand, Bill led them off to one side of the oak tree, not toward the area of the small wooden cross surrounded by flowers that were just starting to poke up through the warm April ground.

"Miz Ophelia wanted the tree planted over there instead of over here next to the coffin," he said. "She didn't want the coffin disturbed by the roots as the tree grew. The grave is actually over here in this area, but Mrs. Maltby always thought it was over there. That's where she decided the cross and the flowers should be. I didn't think it made any difference, so I never said otherwise."

"How far down did you dig, Bill?"

"Not too far – just a couple feet. It's a metal box about two and a half feet long and about a foot and a half wide, about a foot or so tall. We should be able to find it."

The ground was soft from the spring rains. Marty stayed next to the tractor and watched as his dad pulled two long metal rods and two mallets from behind the seat and handed one of each to Bill. They started in the area Bill identified, methodically driving

77

the rods into the ground with their mallets, then carefully marking where they had been so they didn't cover the same area twice. Marty felt a chill when he heard the dull thud of metal hitting metal. It was about ten feet from the tree and the flower bed. There were only two shovels so Marty continued to watch, but curiosity pulled him closer. It didn't take long before the two men pulled up a dirt-encrusted metal box just as Bill described. There was no lock on it. Oblivious to the muddy ground, William Maltby got down on his knees, said a silent prayer, took a deep breath and, while Bill and Marty stood slightly back, opened his son's coffin. It was partially filled with stones and a note – nothing more.

Bill walked forward, took off his hat and scratched his head. "I don't know what to say, William. I never thought for a minute that there was anything other than a deceased child in there. Why would Miz Ophelia do this?"

Marty had inched his way forward just enough to see the contents of the box as well. He was confused. His mind was still trying to fit pieces of a non-conforming puzzle together.

William unfolded the fragile piece of paper, read it silently, and then read it aloud:

My Dear Sister Maria:

If you are reading this, you know that your son is not here. He did not die, at least as of this date. I delivered him to the orphanage on Locust Street, for no other reason than I felt it necessary to do so for your own health and well-being. With William gone and your own health hanging in the balance, and knowing that I will not be here much longer to assist you, I felt it the best thing to do for your sake and for your child's sake. I waited and watched as your baby was taken inside the orphanage, so I know he is in capable hands. I pray that God will keep you in His hands as well so that your health may be restored. Please do not hate me, my precious sister. You will have a difficult road ahead of you as you recover and proceed with your life without William. I know that you cannot possibly work to support yourself plus take care of your home and business, all the while taking care of an infant. This was the only thing I could think of to do for you.

     With love forever,

     Ophelia

Marty could not move. Orphanage. Locust Street. He stood frozen in place while the very real scenario of his birth was unfolding.  His mind was whirling; he felt like he was standing in an artificial world where nothing was real. He vaguely sensed that his dad and Mr. Bill were both looking at him...but he couldn't move.

His father walked over to him and, with tears running down his face, hugged him tightly. The dam broke. Marty, the sensible kid who had never really cried since he was a baby, sobbed. He didn't want to, but he couldn't help himself. Even Bill was crying. Finally, William held his son at arm's length, looking intently into his face.

"You are my son, Marty. You truly are my very own son!"

Marty dried his face with his shirt sleeve. "Yuh," he replied, still trembling and struggling to choke out words. "You are my real dad."

William hugged him again, then pushed him back at arms' length once more and smiled...and then mussed up his hair – and hugged him again! "Come on, you two. Let's get this stuff back on the tractor while we've still got some daylight. You want to drive, Marty? Have we ever got news for your mother!"

He closed the box and left it on the ground, tucked the note in his pocket, and two men, a boy, and a dog climbed aboard, turned away from the oak tree and all that it stood for, and headed for home.

"Congratulations," Bill commented as he shook their hands and slid onto the seat of his old Ford truck. "I am very happy for all of you. This is so unbelievable! Give Maria a hug for me when this is all over, would you, William?"

"Definitely, my friend. Thank you for your help."

***

Maria Maltby was anxiously awaiting the arrival of her husband and son, looking into their faces as they walked into the kitchen. Marty's face was shy but blank, still dazed, trying to absorb all the events of the day. William's face was serious for just a few seconds, slowly changing to a warm smile in anticipation of his wife's reaction.

"Maria, give your son a hug. Give your common-sense, clear-thinking, *biological* son a hug."

Dinner got overdone while Maria read and reread the note from Ophelia. It was her turn to cry, but they were tears of joy. The food may have been hot or it may have been cold – they would never remember nor care. The blessing over dinner took on a deeper and more personal meaning than ever before as they held hands for the first time as a true family. William ended the blessing with: "Thank you God for taking care of our son. Thank you for bringing him home."

Emotions ran the gamut for the Maltby family that night...surprise, shock, disbelief, happiness, anger, resentment, thankfulness, until sheer exhaustion set in. Maria especially went through severe feelings of anger and resentment toward her sister, but ultimately realized that what Ophelia did was what she thought to be best at the time. It was done out of love and concern for Maria and her fragile health and for no other reason. Marty initially dealt with resentment toward someone he never knew, but gratitude in realizing his parents didn't abandon him after all – they had always wanted him and loved him. William dealt with sadness and guilt that his military situation had caused so much harm to his wife and created the separation from their son, but thankfulness and awe that *somehow*, they all found each other.

The next day was spent going through scrapbooks, introducing Marty to his biological family.

"Here is a picture that you will appreciate," his father said. Marty gasped in disbelief as he looked at a picture of his father before he had his teeth fixed. His father – the man with a beautiful, toothy smile, had teeth that were even worse than his. They were not only crooked, they were protruding, overlapping each other. "This is what I looked like when I went into the army," he explained. "With teeth like this, I never wanted to smile with my mouth open, so this is a rare photograph. The army doctor was the one who first told me I had too many teeth for my mouth and I needed to get some pulled. Obviously, there was no time for that with a war going on, but it was one of the first things I did when I 'came back to life' and was sent home. Then I wore braces for a year and I want to tell you, they were doggone uncomfortable! But they were worth it. So my guess is that you have inherited my teeth. It might be worth a trip to the dentist in the near future to hear what he has to say. If he feels braces might help and you want to go through that ordeal someday, we can make it happen."

Marty didn't hesitate. "Not much to think about, Dad. I am ready right now. I am really, really ready!" he answered, reverting back to his usual shy, closed-mouth grin.

Then Maria pointed to one of her pictures. "Here's where you get your red hair, Marty. The camera doesn't show it very well, but your hair is the same color that mine used to be. It matched my freckles very well, just like yours does. I never liked it, but thankfully I have a wonderful hairdresser who toned it down. My guess is that you're not going to be interested in that solution, however.

"But mine isn't red, Mom, it's orange."

Maria smiled. "Well, yes, *it is* kind of orangey red, and so was mine, and I do understand how you feel. I also appreciate the fact that your father loved me even with orangey-red hair and freckles. And think about what a boring world this would be if everyone looked alike. You and I are just unique, that's all. Here – I'll match you freckle for freckle." She pulled up her sleeve and put her arm next to Marty's. Yup, they matched!

"And you should also remember, Maria," William chimed in, "that you liked me even with my bad teeth!"

"Now I feel very special," Marty laughed. "I've got all that stuff."

They all enjoyed poking fun at themselves and laughing. Then Maria Maltby chuckled with yet another amusing thought: "Can you imagine what we are going to go through down at the courthouse when we try to get all this paperwork straightened out? Just think – we are going to walk in there with a twelve-year-old death certificate that we need to cancel because our son never died, an adoption certificate that we want to cancel because we adopted our own son, and then try to explain how our son grew up ten miles away and we never recognized him or knew how he got there. Then we can tell them how Marty figured out who he really was because of a blanket and attended the opening of his own coffin to see if he and his blanket were in there. Oh, yes. It's going to be an interesting day!"

And indeed, it was! It *did* take a lot of time, paperwork, explaining, and patience. When they left the courthouse, the death certificate and adoption certificate were cancelled, but there was still confusion about how to treat the legal name change from Marty L. Smith, the name he had known all his life, to his new name of Marty William Maltby, especially since his birth certificate said his name was Martin Calvin Maltby. The "Calvin" was after his father's father.

# THE UGLY POPCORN TREE

The best story of all, however, was how they found each other again. The local newspaper took credit, of course. They felt it was because they offered a new category and prize to the Maltbys' Christmas Tree Decorating Contest: "The Ugliest Popcorn Tree."

But was that *really* how it came about? Or was it because Maria and William Maltby extended their love for children to include a whole community? Or maybe it was Mrs. Rose's ongoing care for the orphans at Barclay and taking advantage of an opportunity on their behalf. Or could it have been Mrs. Rose's scrapbook project that she meticulously maintained for each of the children? Perhaps it was a protective sister wrapping a baby in a blanket that she created with love as he was given to the care of others. Or maybe it was the ingenuity of four orphans well past an adoptable age who thoughtfully watched over the younger children in their orphanage and wanted to win a special popcorn treat for them.

**OR** could it all have been part of something bigger?

...Perhaps an unexplainably warm 80-degree day in Pennsylvania in December, with a sun so hot that it infused heat on a supposedly ugly tree?

...Could it have been "coincidentally" helped by a fire pit meant for toasting marshmallows that heated their tree even more, turning its decorations into explosive attention-getters?

...Or could it have been "just the right time" for the life paths of three people to cross again in a special way and a special place?

# THE TRUTH

Surely God wouldn't really use twine, brown paper, glue, a mish-mash of discarded hair, black paint and an ugly popcorn tree contest to reunite a family, would He?

Why not?

Who is more unique than God?

# A Brief History of the Orphan Trains

- From 1854 to 1929, an estimated 250,000 orphaned, abandoned, and homeless children were placed in homes throughout the United States and Canada during the Orphan Train Movement. Over 30,000 were taken from the streets of New York City alone.
- Some were true orphans with no parents or family to take care of them. Others were "half" orphans who lost one parent and the other parent could not take care of them. Some were runaways trying to escape abuse, neglect, abandonment, or drugs.
- There was also massive overpopulation in the New York City area in the mid-nineteenth century due to extensive immigration. Some families were very large and parents simply could not feed or care for all of their children.
- Orphan Trains were started by a Congressional Minister, the Rev. Charles Loring Brace of the New York Children's Aid Society.
- It was the beginning of documented foster care in America.
- It eventually led to a host of child welfare reforms, including child labor laws, official adoption, and the establishment of proper foster care services.
- Poor and orphaned children living in New York City were resettled with farm families in The West to deter them from a life of crime and poverty and to help with labor needed on farms where population was low.

- The first train went out from The Children's Aid Society on September 20, 1854, with 46 ten-to-twelve-year-old boys and girls. Their destination was Dowagiac, Michigan. All 46 children were successfully placed in new homes.
- Children who were not true orphans were not put on the trains until a "release for placement" was signed by whatever family member was available.
- Westbound journeys began in New York City, Boston, and other coastal cities. The trains stopped at more than 45 states across the country as well as Canada and Mexico.
- Children were taken in groups of 40 with two agents from the Children's Aid Society.
- Notices went out to key cities in advance of the train's arrival of "Homes Wanted for Orphans."
- When the trains stopped, the children were taken from the depot and displayed in a local theater where they were put up on stage – thus the saying, "up for adoption."
- Often brothers and sisters were separated by the adoption process, sometimes never to see each other again. This was mitigated somewhat later on with the placing agent put in a position of responsibility to stay apprised of the welfare of the children. If it became obvious that the placement was not a good match, or if the agent felt the child was being abused, he or she would remove the child from its adopted home and try to find another family.
- In 1869, the Sisters of Charity of St. Vincent de Paul created the Catholic Charities of New York to receive abandoned newborn babies. This led to "mercy trains" or "baby trains" specifically for very young orphans. They worked in conjunction with Priests in the Midwest and South to place the

babies in Catholic homes although their religious upbringing was turned over to the adoptive family.

- The orphan trains came to an end by 1930 when the depression made it extremely hard for families to provide for additional children. Plus, laws were being put into place that made it harder for children to be uprooted. Instead, foster homes started replacing the larger orphanages and institutions.
- It is estimated that over 200 million people today are descendants of an orphan train rider.

# *Notable Orphans & Adoptees*

Maya Angelou
Lance Armstrong
Louis Armstrong
Johann Sebastian Bach
Tallulah Bankhead
L. L. Bean
Ingrid Bergman
Simon Bolivar
Aaron Burr
Richard Burton
Augustus Caesar
Truman Capote
George Washington Carver
Ray Charles
President Bill Clinton
Nat King Cole
Bo Diddley
Ella Fitzgerald
President Gerald Ford
Jamie Foxx
Newt Gingrich
Alexander Hamilton
John Hancock
Faith Hill
Herbert Hoover
President Andrew Jackson
Steve Jobs
John Keats
Eartha Kitt
John Lennon
Art Linkletter
George Lopez
Lee Majors

Nelson Mandela
Marilyn Monroe
Moses*
Edgar Allan Poe
Priscilla Presley
Nancy Reagan
Eleanor Roosevelt
Babe Ruth
Bessie Smith
Barbara Stanwyck
Ice-T
Dave Thomas
Jim Thorpe
J. R. R. Tolkien
Leo Tolstoy
Ruth Westheimer

*Yes, even Moses was considered an orphan by Biblical scholars. His parents gave him up to save his life. Pharaoh's daughter found him in the reeds and, assuming him to be an orphan, adopted him and raised him as her own son.

# About the Author

## Madelyn Rohrer

Born in Upstate New York, Madelyn currently resides in Northeast Tennessee – via Canada and Southern California. She grew up as a "border kid," having lived on both sides of the U.S.-Canadian border and in Southern California just five miles from the Mexican border.

Following a career in Corporate America plus owning her own office management company and sharing in a family-owned business, she is now pursuing her personal interests of history, the antique car hobby, music, involvement with her church, public speaking, storytelling, and writing.

Madelyn was introduced to storytelling in 1996 after moving to Jonesborough, Tennessee, the home of storytelling international, and signing on as a storytelling tour guide in the historic district. It led to a second career as a professional storyteller and published author. Although her portfolio of oral and written stories is diverse, her favorites are those that inspire, strengthen moral values, and make history fun. Her stories are suitable for all audiences.

# Madelyn's Books

Her first book, *Tiggy Touch Wood*, was published in 2014 and includes ten original short stories composed for the storytelling stage and subsequently converted to written form. The book has received excellent reviews from the storytelling and literary communities, including a 5-star award from Red City Review. Several stories have been chosen for writers' guild anthologies.

*Shoes in the River,* a novel, was released in 2015. It presents an insight into real life in China as affected by the one-child-per-family edict, which produced a world-wide dilemma still being dealt with today. The characters are fictional but the issues are real. It has received excellent reviews from Red City Review and Writers Digest. The sequel is scheduled for a 2020 completion.

*The Ugly Popcorn Tree* (2018) is a novella of true-to-life fiction concerning older orphans ("tweens"), some of the circumstances that would have them lingering in an orphanage at an older age, and the difficulties they encounter while waiting for their new homes and parents.

***Touched by Tennessee, Second Edition***
(copyright 2016; second edition 2020) is a
collection of eight short stories, originally told on
stage. They are true historical stories with the
common thread of the State of Tennessee. One of
the stories was chosen as a first-place winner by
*Storytelling World Awards*, a publication of the
National Storytelling Network. Also available as
an audio book.

# Children's Books

***Hobie the Christmas Spider*** (2017) is the first in
"The Critter Series" of children's books. It is
created from a bit of Germanic folklore and an
Old-World Tradition of sharing Christmas Eve
with the animals…only from the perspective of
the spiders. It teaches children about the love
Jesus has for all living creatures, even the tiniest
of all. It is a story of the "magic" of Christmas.

***Bert the Owl Bat*** (2019) is the second in "The
Critter Series" of children's books. Join Bert as
he meets a new but unlikely (and scary) friend
quite by chance. Bert and his friend are leery of
each other at first but soon decide in their minds
to be friends. When their lives are interrupted by
danger, their bond of friendship becomes one of
the heart.

# Other Publications

***Johnny Come Back*** (2018) is a true story of an East Tennessee couple. When Claudia, a seasoned emergency room nurse, takes her husband to the hospital on Christmas Eve 2017 with flu-like symptoms, they don't return home for eighty-four days. This is their amazing story as they lived it. (Written for them by Madelyn Rohrer).

For more information on any of Madelyn's books, including available formats and how to order, log on to her website at:

www.storytellermadelynrohrer.com

...or visit her YouTube channel at www.YouTube.com and search for *Stories by Madelyn Rohrer.*

# Bibliography

7 Historical Figures Who Grew Up as Orphans:
www.history.com/news/history-lists/7-historical-figures-
who-grew-up-as-orphans

19 Celebrities Who Were Orphaned as Children:
www.ranker.com/list/famous-orphans/celebrity-lists

Marilyn Monroe, Steve Jobs, and 6 Other Famous Orphans
Who Helped Change the World:
www.owlcation.com/humanities/Eight-Famous-People-You-
Didn't-Know-Were-Orphans

30 Famous People Who Were Adopted:
www.shophope.org/2014/03/10/30-famous-people-adopted

13 Famous People Who Were Adopted:
www.entertainment.howstuffworks.com/13_famous_people

National Orphan Train Complex:
www.orphantraindepot.org/history/

The Orphan Train Movement:
www.childrensaidnyc.org/about/orphan-train-movement

Orphan Trains:
www.ancestry.com/orphan_trains

Lost Children: Riders on the Orphan Train:

www.neh.gov/humanities/2007/novemberdecember/feature/lost-children

A History of the Orphan Trains:

www.Kancoll.org/articles/orphans/

www.ingramcontent.com/pod-product-compliance
Lightning Source LLC
Chambersburg PA
CBHW020626130626
46552CB00003B/1105